A Treasure's Trove

Secrets
of the
Alchemist Dar

1 2 3 4 5 6 7 8 9 18 19 15 11 23 12 14

20 10 13 22 21 16 17 24

A Treasure's Trove

Secrets of the Alchemist Dar

A fantasy for everyone!

Written and Illustrated

by

Treasure Trove, Inc.
New Canaan, CT

Treasure Trove, Inc.

Production	**Artist/Studio Manager**	**Artist**
Christopher Goncalves	Brian Kammerer	Brent Bully

To everyone who reads this with a child

Illustrations copyright © 2006 Michael Stadther

Published by Treasure Trove, Inc.
New Canaan, CT 06840
Distributed by Simon Scribbles,
an imprint of Simon & Schuster, Inc.
New York, NY 10020

Simon Scribbles and
colophon are trademarks of
Simon & Schuster, Inc.

Copyright © 2006 Treasure Trove, Inc.

Editorial Consultant
Gene Hult
Design Consultant
Jennifer Laino

Visit www.alchemistdar.com for information on the treasure hunt.

ISBN-13: 978-0-9760618-7-8 (HC)
ISBN-10: 0-9760618-7-2 (HC)

ISBN-13: 978-0-9760618-8-5 (PBK)
ISBN-10: 0-9760618-8-0 (PBK)

Manufactured in the United States of America

First Edition
2 4 6 8 10 9 7 5 3 1

Contents

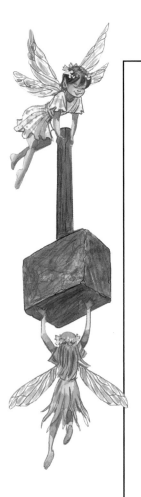

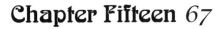

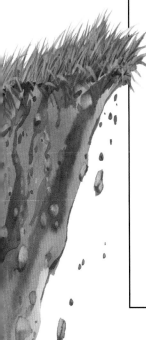

Preface

This story takes place in a mythical forest at some unknown time, either in the past or the future. It tells of Zac, a handsome woodcarver, his beautiful half-elf, half-human wife Ana, and their two trusty half-dog, half-moth doths.

The story also tells about the Fairy Rings of Eternal Life worn on chains around the necks of Good Fairies that keep them from dying or getting old; and how one of the evil Dark Fairies, who do get old and die, plots to get the rings by killing the Good Fairies.

It is a fantasy story of love, adventure, and mystery—a real mystery that includes you!

The mystery begins with clues concealed in the pages of this book that will give anyone anywhere in the world who can read English a chance to solve the clues and obtain one of the one hundred real diamond rings valued together at more than US$2,000,000.

The rings are all made by the world famous jeweler Aaron Basha and are set with various red, blue, pink, yellow, and white diamonds.

Anyone can look for clues in this book, solve the clues, and, if he or she meets all the requirements in the Official Rules printed in the back of *Secrets of the Alchemist Dar*, be awarded a ring.

In my previous bestselling treasure hunt book *A Treasure's Trove* I hid solid gold tokens around the continental United States. When found by solving clues in the book, the tokens were redeemed for more than US$1,000,000 in real jewels.*

This time, however, I don't tell you what I have hidden, where to go, who to see, or how to get your ring—you have to figure out everything for yourself.

As before, nothing is hidden in dangerous or remote locations. Nothing is buried and nothing is hidden on private property, in caves, or underwater. Take no risks looking for anything associated with this treasure hunt, don't disturb or move anything, and obey all laws.

Once again, I believe the clues are solvable and I hope you get a ring.

I also hope you take the time to read this story with a child and discover the wonderful secrets in this book. I believe you will enjoy the story more if you first flip the book over, turn it upside down, and look through the *Book of Dark Spells* (just the way the characters do in the story) to see if you can find any of its secrets.

Happy hunting!

Michael Stadther

* The solutions to the clues in *A Treasure's Trove* (ISBN-13: 978-0-9760618-2-3 and ISBN-10: 0-9760618-0-5) are described with the finders' stories in the *Official Solution Book to A Treasure's Trove* (ISBN-13: 978-0-9760618-5-4 and ISBN-10: 0-9760618-5-6).

Syzygy

Prologue
The First Eclipse: The Syzygy

High above the bedroom in the tree house Zac had built for Ana, his bride of almost two years, as they lay sleeping with their trusty, chubby doth, Pook, tucked under the covers, a celestial dance was being performed—a slow rotating dance, a dance that never ceased. Although the dance had never happened this way before, it had been destined to be performed this way since the beginning of time.

That night, as Ana lay safe in Zac's arms, secure in Yorah's mighty oak branches, she dreamed of her wedding anniversary approaching in two days. Zac slept soundly, pleasantly tired from carrying a new load of his hand-carved wooden boxes to the village earlier that day. Pook slept lightly, his guard-dog sense keeping him half awake even though his moth sense had told him to close his eyes once the lights were out.

A cool night breeze brushed over the Good Fairies that slept in Yorah's leaves: the gentle Flower Fairies, the clumsy Kootenstoopits, and the mischievous Pickensrooters.

The Great Forest was peaceful that night.

No one dreamt the Dark Fairies—the Darklings, the evil, destructive malcontents who caused pestilence and disease—would soon leave their black cave again. The Darklings had not ventured out for almost a year, since Zac and the brave Pook had destroyed their leader.

None of the peaceful sleepers could know far away, deep in the Grotto, a new leader was emerging to unleash the Darklings into the Great Forest. The sleepers couldn't know they would be forced to leave the Great Forest. They couldn't know all the Good Fairies soon would die.

Nor could they anticipate how the new, evil Darkling leader and the celestial dance of the sun and the moon with the Earth would cause all these things to happen.

Everyone slept peacefully as the celestial spheres started their inevitable alignment, the Earth almost directly between the sun and the moon. The shadow of the Earth—now just touching the edge of the moon—soon would cover the lunar orb. This would be the first of three eclipses to occur over the Great Forest.

As the inhabitants of the Great Forest slept, the first eclipse, the alignment of sun, moon, and Earth—the syzygy—had begun.

Chapter 1

The First Eclipse: The Moon Disappears

During the tranquil night, Dragonfly, the Air Group Leader for the Forest Creatures, patrolled the Great Forest as he did every night, watching the mouth of the cave where the Darklings lived.

The mountain containing the cave had recovered from the blight that had infected it a year ago and was once again the most beautiful part of the Great Forest. Dragonfly soared in the cool night air over the clear stream that spilled from the cave's mouth and splashed down the lush mountain, trickling over moss-covered limestone rocks.

Dragonfly was pleased to see that the evil Dark Fairies were still afraid to venture out of the cave. They hadn't left their cramped quarters for a year since Pook almost died destroying their leader.

He could see hundreds of Darklings holding fiery torches, crammed into the mouth of the cave so tightly that the mass of foul bodies moved in ripples like a single living organism.

If the Darklings remained there, the other inhabitants of the Great Forest would be free from the diseases, pestilence, and destruction they caused. Dragonfly also watched a red-gray shadow spreading across the face of the moon, making it seem to disappear.

Despite the unusual lunar event tonight, all seemed well to Dragonfly.

Chapter 2

The Alchemist Dar

In the packed black hole of malcontents, near the cave mouth, swaying with the dark mass of bodies, staring out at the shadow growing on the moon, stood Dar, the last of the Malic Hest Darklings.

The Malic Hest, an order of especially vile Darklings, spilled chemicals and potions causing all manner of destruction. They studied to be alchemists; they experimented with acids and chemicals in vain attempts to transmute lead to gold and change the ordinary into the extraordinary. They were also direct descendants of the Hest, as were Good Fairies, elves, and other Darklings. Yet they wanted more than the other fairies—they wanted to be as powerful as the Hest, who once cared for the Great Forest.

The Malic Hest were also taller than most Dark Fairies, and arguably, more intelligent. They rarely flew since their brittle wings usually broke early in life, and they frequently befriended Pale Drophidians—transparent serpents which looked fierce, but were, in fact, as light as air—to carry them through the sky.

Like all Dark Fairies, the Malic Hest chose a life of evil against all the other inhabitants of the Great Forest. They especially hated the Good Fairies and coveted the Fairy Rings of Eternal Life that hung from the Good Fairies' necks under their garments.

With the start of the three syzygies, Dar would soon fulfill his alchemist training to defeat the Good Fairies and claim their rings.

"Dar see syzygy," he said under his breath. "Syzygy see Dar," he mumbled, repeating his thoughts backward as was the custom of the Malic Hest.

"Dar knows secret," he whispered. "Secret knows Dar. Secret book. Book secret," he said sinisterly. "*Book of Dark Spells*. Spells dark of book."

The book had been stolen by the evil Malic Hest from the last Hest, Kiem Rethdast, when the book was known as the *Book of Light Spells*. The Malic Hest wanted the book to create their own Fairy Rings of Eternal Life. They ripped the book apart for its secrets and changed the book for their vile purposes into the *Book of Dark Spells*. But they never succeeded in understanding the ancient Hest language and many of the mysteries hidden in the book by the Hest.

Now the book lay deep in the cave, past where any other Darkling ventured.

Dar snatched a lit torch from a smaller Darkling and pushed his way through the packed crowd deeper into the cave. He shuffled stiffly on his stubby legs as if they were table legs. His brittle, tattered, broken wings, unsuitable for flying, twitched, revealing his glee. He elbowed his way through the mass of bodies, climbing and crawling over them when there was no other way through, traveling deeper into the cave—into parts where only he and his Malic Hest teachers had been.

"Dar knows about three eclipses. Eclipses three about knows Dar," he mumbled as he plodded down the dark cave path.

"Dar get *Book of Dark Spells*. Spells dark of book get Dar."

It was the time of the syzygies—the first of three consecutive eclipses—the time Dar had been trained for in his youth. Now, during the first eclipse, he would cast a powerful spell in the book to release the Dark Fairies from the cave. With the next eclipse, he would destroy the crops and food—forcing the humans to leave the forest. With the third eclipse, he would cast the final spell to kill the Good Fairies and get their rings for the Darklings.

"It is time. Time is it," he said under his breath.

Dar entered a narrow, descending passage. He slid down the damp tunnel—almost losing his grip on the torch—to the lowest level in the cave, deep under the mountain.

The tunnel exited into a large vaulted chamber with tall columns of water-carved limestone. The stone columns seemed to dance in the light from his flickering torch, looking like graceful blue and pink waterfalls spilling from dark shadows above him.

At the far end of the chamber, he squeezed through a winding path cut through the limestone walls. After several feet, the path ended at a pool of water—an apparent dead end.

"Dar knows about room. Room about knows Dar," he mumbled as he wedged the torch into a small crevice.

"Secret room. Room secret." He slipped into the water, unconcerned with the pitch blackness of the liquid. "Hold his breath. Breath his hold," he said anxiously to himself, as he sank beneath the surface.

Then, as he had done long ago, he felt his way along the underwater wall and exited to a new chamber through a hole below the surface, entering a hidden room—the alchemist's chamber.

He surfaced within the musty room, its walls aglow from blue and green shimmering vials of chemicals and potions mixed ages ago by his Malic Hest instructors, and pulled himself out of the water onto the limestone floor.

He stared at the old things within the chamber. He hadn't been here since his training as an apprentice alchemist. It was where he had studied the *Book of Dark Spells*.

The room hadn't changed. Vaulted limestone arches carved by dripping water for thousands of centuries loomed overhead, the silence only broken by drops of water falling from the high ceiling.

In the middle of the chamber stood a wooden desk covered in faded manuscripts and vellum scrolls, many containing strange symbols that even Dar couldn't understand. On top of the scrolls were the old ink quills, pots, and magnifying glasses that the Malic Hest had used to try to interpret and change the *Book of Light Spells* they stole from the Hest.

In the middle of all the faded papers and curious instruments lay the *Book of Dark Spells*. Dar grabbed the book and hugged it happily.

"Time it is. Is it time. Hurry. Hurry," he yelped, his words echoing through the chamber.

He removed his tunic and wrapped it tightly around the old book.

He couldn't linger; he had to get back to the cave entrance before the eclipse was over so he could recite the first Eclipse Spell.

He slipped back into the water and surfaced into the light at the edge of the winding path where he had left his torch. After crawling and pushing his way to the entrance of the cave, he finally stood at the cave mouth, under the darkening moon.

Moments from the peak of the eclipse, Dar opened the book, pointed to the moon, and screamed the first lines of the spell of Open Fairies Dark.

"Fairies in the cave, I command you all." Dar recoiled as if punched in the stomach by an invisible force. The spell's wind that would suck the Dark Fairies out of the cave was starting to affect the caster.

Following the blow, he collected himself and prepared to read the next line of the spell, pleased that he would soon release the Darklings back into the Great Forest.

The shadow of the Earth moved further across the face of the moon and the night darkened as the eclipse continued. With the moon in full shadow, perfectly aligned with the Earth and the sun, the eclipse reached its peak, the moon almost invisible in the night sky.

Dar rotated the book to read the next two lines of the spell.

"Take flight now leave and heed my call," he shouted at the top of his lungs.

Again the invisible force attacked him, this time knocking him to the cave floor.

The spell took effect. As if pulled by winds that could not be resisted, thousands of Dark Fairies were whisked from the cave and spread to all parts of the Great Forest, ready to collect the rings from the Good Fairies.

The first syzygy had ended; Dar's first spell had been cast.

Chapter 3
The Dragonfly

"Condition Red, Condition Red!" shouted Dragonfly as he buzzed high over the cave, watching the evil throngs of Dark Fairies spreading throughout the land.

He wanted to attack them, but he was hopelessly outnumbered. Instead, he sped away from the empty cave, back toward the Linden Stump, to alert his fellow Forest Creatures.

Tonight he had witnessed an evil Darkling reading from an old book and screaming at the night sky. He had watched as the Darklings were released back into the Great Forest, and he had seen the moon disappear.

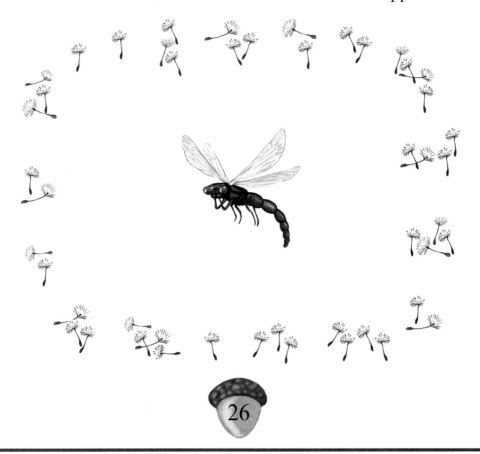

Chapter 4
The Dream

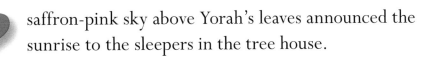

A saffron-pink sky above Yorah's leaves announced the sunrise to the sleepers in the tree house.

Zac awoke first and sensed his lovely bride lying beside him. He also felt his chubby, loyal doth Pook sleeping by his feet under the covers. He watched his wife's peaceful sleep, her gentle breathing. Zac thought she was the most beautiful halfling girl he had ever seen. Her human features were complemented by her delicate elf eyes and ears, inherited from her elf mother.

He wondered about her dream. Perhaps she dreamed of him, perhaps of their wedding anniversary tomorrow.

This was the perfect time to listen to her thoughts. He could discover what she wanted for her anniversary. He hadn't learned to hear her thoughts as well as she wanted, but he wasn't a halfling, he was just a human—a woodcarver. Try as he might, he could only hear his wife's thoughts if he really opened his mind, thinking of nothing. A peek into her dream should be easy while she slept.

Zac leaned onto his side, closed his eyes, and cleared his mind. Soon, as if a fog lifted, he could see Ana's dream as if it were in his own mind. He could see an image of Yorah's tree roots where he had first seen Ana, where he had proposed, and where he had first kissed her.

The moment was just as he remembered. He could see how nervously he plucked a clover blossom and formed it into a ring, making a small slit in the stem near the blossom and tucking the stem end into it. He could see how he placed it on her finger. When he asked her to marry him, she accepted eagerly, throwing her arms around him. Though the meager blossom wouldn't last, she admired it as if it were the most beautiful engagement ring in the world.

Then her dream changed. Zac now saw dark shapes moving within Yorah's limbs and roots—formless, shadowy figures. He sensed Ana's dread. Her halfling senses revealed the future. Her dream changed again. Now she dreamed of Pook in a fierce battle with one of the shadowy figures, and she imagined the doth falling into a deep hole, disappearing forever. Zac shuddered as she dreamed of death.

Ana stirred, her dream broken by the brightening dawn light. Zac gently held her, contemplating awakening her with a kiss. He brought his lips close to hers.

At that very instant, Pook shot out from his warm sleeping place under the covers, stuck his broad head between the lovers, smiled, *uffed*, and announced himself with his namesake, a quiet *pook*, releasing the foul odor.

That did it. Everyone was awake, the lovers' mood broken by the stinky smell.

"Oh, Zac!" Ana complained. "He's such a stinky thing. Why can't he behave like other doths?"

But Pook couldn't be like other doths. He was chubby and gentle.
He loved lying in the sun, having his belly rubbed, and stuffing himself
with purple thistles. Yet he always barked bravely at the tool-stealing
grubinmoles, cawcats, and tam-o'jacks that lurked in the Great Forest,
and he would protect Zac and Ana with his life.

It didn't really matter to Ana or Zac that Pook's wings were too small for
him to fly well, or that he was fat and stinky. She and Zac loved him.

And he loved them back.

Chapter 5

The Alarm

ater the same morning, near the birch grove far from the tree house and the Grotto, Air Group Leader Dragonfly arrived at the Linden Stump where the Forest Creatures slept. He intended to report his alarming observations of last night to Spider, the Ground Forces Leader, once he could awaken the troops. He and Spider would then lead the other Forest Creatures in an attack on the Dark Fairy who unleashed the Darklings. Together they would save the forest.

"Red alert! Red alert!" he shouted as he buzzed in for a landing.

Inside the stump, Ant awoke first, bleary-eyed and hungry, as usual. "Red dessert? Sure," he said with a yawn. "I'll have some red dessert."

Hearing Ant's comments about dessert, Snail awoke next. "Oh . . . ," he began excitedly and slowly, unable to finish his thought quickly.

Ever alert, Hummingbird hummed approvingly, hovering above the other Forest Creatures.

"Dessert?" asked boisterous Rhinoceros Beetle, awakening slowly. "Anytime is fine for red dessert . . . but, uh . . . uh, what the heck is red dessert? Is it strawberries? I love strawberries. But I don't like those seedy things that get stuck in my mandibles. Maybe it's cherries. But they have that big pit.

"Heck, I don't care what color it is; I just love dessert," he declared with a big belly laugh.

"How de-lec-ta-ble," said scholarly Caterpillar, pronouncing his words distinctly as if he were an English professor. "We shall feast together, in fine style, on the de-ssert that Dragonfly has brought us. I shall pre-pare the table."

". . . boy . . ." said Snail with a broad smile, proud of himself for finishing his thought, anticipating a sweet treat. "I love . . ."

"Hush, all of you. It's not dessert," said the sleepy, matronly Ladybug calmly. "It's just an alert. Go back to sleep all of you." And she closed her eyes.

"Alert?" she cried a moment later, her eyes popping wide, realizing what Dragonfly had said. "Oh dear, it's an alert!" she screamed. "Somebody, do something!"

That did it. Everyone was awake.

"We don't get any dessert?" complained Ant. "What kind of a place is this? You know there are other Linden Stumps in the forest we could eat at."

"You mean, *at* which we could eat," said Caterpillar, correcting Ant's grammar.

"Yeah, at which we could eat at."

"Do we get zzzomething zzzweet?" buzzed Bee. "I like zzzweet thingzzz zzzooo much!" He hugged himself and looked skyward, swaying from side to side, dreaming of sweet honey.

"Eat? Is that all you think about?" asked Spider, slathering her words with saliva. "I have plenty to eat hanging in the back. All we have to do is unwrap something."

"You betcha, octo-eyes," said Rhinoceros Beetle with a second belly laugh. "Food is all you think about if your heart beats as fast as Hummingbird's!"

Hummingbird hummed approvingly.

Caterpillar spoke again, "Mayhap you should all con-cen-trate on the ahh-lert rather than de-ssert."

"Hush, all of you," Ladybug ordered. "Listen to Dragonfly's report."

The group had finally calmed down from the false breakfast claims when Snail finished his thought, ". . . red dessert. Whew."

"Dessert?" shouted the excited Ant again at the mention of the word.

The Forest Creatures erupted with more cries of hunger.

"Listen up, you bugs!" shouted Dragonfly. "We have a Level One breach of security at the cave."

Ladybug wasn't sure what a Level One breach of security was, but she sensed it was serious and shushed the others.

Dragonfly began his speech in his usual dramatic, militant fashion and told the Creatures about an evil Dark Fairy who read from an old book, releasing the Darklings into the night, and he told them about how the moon turned red and then disappeared.

The Forest Creatures gasped and trembled, afraid of the evil Darklings.

"Oh, my!" shrieked Ladybug. "What should we do about this new Darkling leader?"

"Well," said Spider menacingly, "I could tie him up and hang him up." She rolled her eight eyes skyward, thinking, "Then on a rainy day we could eat him up."

"No," Ladybug said firmly. "We can't take on all the Dark Fairies. We need a plan!"

"A plan?" barked the Dragonfly. "We don't need a plan. We need to attack!"

"No," Ladybug said. "We shall go tell Yorah, the wisest oak tree in the forest. She will help us. She will tell us what to do."

They all agreed and off they flew. Hummingbird carried Grasshopper perched on his back, Ant rode atop Butterfly, Bee held on to Snail, Spider rode on Dragonfly, and heavy Caterpillar was carried by the Firefly and Beetle. Flying alone, Ladybug led the way.

Chapter 6

The Morning of the Day Before the Anniversary

he residents of the tree house were all awake, preparing for the day.

Ana sat on the edge of the bed, brushing her long auburn hair, singing with the Flower Fairies gathered around her.

To Zac, it was just another meaningless song with strange Flower Fairy words, but he hummed along merrily.

Zac searched through his dresser drawer for his favorite tan checkered socks. When he spied them, one seemed to be alive, moving slowly within the larger pile. Then it withdrew deeper into the drawer, disappearing entirely. "Hmmm," said Zac. He pulled at the other still visible sock. It didn't budge. Pulling harder, he finally managed to yank it from the drawer. On the end of the sock hung a tiny Kootenstoopit wearing the other tan sock on its head.

Zac plucked his sock from the fairy's head, pointed a menacing finger at the Kootenstoopit, and the tiny creature begrudgingly let go and flew off.

"These darn fairies are into everything," he said exasperatedly, placing the socks beside him on the bed.

He sat on the edge of the bed and prepared to put on his socks. No sooner had he crossed his legs to put on a sock than from underneath him erupted a jabbering and wiggling of tiny arms, legs, and wings. Startled, Zac stood up, while a clearly annoyed Pickensrooter shot out from the bedcovers.

The Pickensrooter jabbered nonsense and hovered near Zac's head. Zac tried his best to shoo it away, but it was no use—the nimble little fairy darted around easily, avoiding every swipe. Then it zipped across the chest of drawers, knocking bottles and boxes out of its way.

"Sometimes I wish I had never started believing in fairies so I wouldn't see them," Zac said to the laughing Ana.

"Having trouble?" she purred coyly. "They just want to play."

Zac responded with something that sounded like "harrumph!"

Then he sat back on the bed and reached for the place where he had left the socks just in time to see another Kootenstoopit disappearing under the bed, pulling both socks with it.

Zac lunged across the bed, reaching for the socks. Just before they vanished, he pulled them back. One in each hand, he stood, held out his arms, and stared at two giggling Kootenstoopits, one hanging on the end of each sock. He shook the socks but the fairies held fast.

"Arrrgh! How can I get anything done with these fairies undoing everything I do?" he asked. "Isn't there something you can do to help me? They're *your* friends."

Ana laughed again. "Oh, all right. I'll help the big strong woodcarver."

She stood up, crossed her arms over her chest, and stomped her foot firmly. Dozens of fairies hidden under the bedcovers, in the open sock drawer, in Zac's boot—everywhere, it seemed—flew out of the room as fast as they could.

"There," she said, smiling. "Think you can get dressed by yourself now?"

"Harrumph," Zac said again and sat to put on his socks and boots.

Finally, he stood, fully dressed in his favorite green shirt, brown trousers held up by fine green suspenders buttoned in the front and back, socks, and leather boots. He held out his arms, displaying himself for his wife to see, as if he had finished an impossible chore.

She smiled, pleased, and nodded toward him, as if dressing himself deserved her admiration.

With his arms still held out, Zac sang, "Ta-da!" as if he had completed a feat of magic. Almost simultaneously, two tiny Kootenstoopits, unnoticed by Zac, hovered in front of him and completed the unraveling of the thread securing the two buttons on the front of the suspenders holding up his pants. As they flew away with his buttons, with Ana laughing uncontrollably, Zac's pants fell to his ankles.

Chapter 7
The Clover Blossom Ring

ater that day, while Zac worked in his workshop, Ana prepared his lunch.

Ana sang with several of the Flower Fairies who were sitting in a circle on the kitchen table while she prepared Zac's favorite Marmo'elk and potato stew. If she could give him a big enough portion, she could hide some broccoli under the stew where he wouldn't notice it and maybe he would eat it. She didn't always approve of his simple woodcarver eating habits and she wished he would eat more vegetables.

As Ana prepared the plate, one of Yorah's many knothole faces watched.

"How is the new chrysalis, dearie?" asked Yorah, referring to the doth chrysalis—the cocoon—that had appeared several weeks ago hanging outside of Zac's workshop window.

"The new doth should emerge any time now, Yorah," Ana said. "It's so exciting but we still haven't picked a name. It looks big—much bigger than Pook. I told Zac that he can pick the name."

"Have you told him what you want for your wedding anniversary tomorrow?" Yorah asked.

"No, Yorah, I haven't," Ana replied. "I'm hoping he will pick what I really want without me telling him what it is."

"Well, sweetie, he is a hardheaded man and you know he's not very good at hearing your thoughts," Yorah reminded her.

"Yes, I know," Ana said, "but I hope he gets me an anniversary ring—even a simple one. He was so poor when he proposed to me he couldn't even afford an engagement ring. The clover ring he made for me dried up and just blew away."

Chapter 8
The New Doth

It was midday, and in his workshop Zac was making a tea box for one of the women in the village. The sun shone through Yorah's leaves, shafts of light bouncing off Zac's woodworking tools.

As Zac sat at his workbench, the fairies continued to torment him. The Flower Fairies sang nonsense songs that he didn't understand. The Kootenstoopits tugged on his socks, pulling them down. The Pickensrooters opened and closed the boxes around the workshop, smashing the lids shut with as loud a bang as possible. Most annoying of all, they sneaked in at night and rearranged his tools just to bother him.

Even with these petty annoyances, it had been a good year in the workshop. The bins were filled with fine aged hardwoods and the shelves were stacked with maple hatboxes, cherry spice boxes, toy blocks for the children in the village, and fine inlaid wooden jewelry boxes of paddock and bubinga.

Pook lay on his back on the floor at Zac's feet, his legs skyward, his tiny mothlike wings tucked under him, basking in the warmth of a sunbeam. Contented with his warm belly, he ignored the fairies and lightly dozed.

Zac looked at him lovingly. He would never forget how the once-timid doth had saved his life from the last leader of the Dark Fairies. Pook puffed a little *uff*, not wanting to expend the effort for a full bark. Zac smiled. He loved Pook's broad grin and his gentle nature, and he always laughed out loud whenever Pook tried to fly, his chubby body struggling to stay aloft more than a few feet, his legs and tiny wings spreading awkwardly in all directions.

As Ana entered the workshop with Zac's lunch, she stopped to watch him cut the dovetail joint for the back of the box. She admired his strong hands as he sawed through thick wood planks—hands that could be so gentle when he made the delicate inlaid curves on the top of the box. She wondered if she could ever make such a beautiful object.

STADTHER '06 KAMMERER

Zac had smelled the Marmo'elk and potato stew, so he knew it was coming. He hoped that Ana hadn't hidden any vegetables in it as she usually did. He knew she wanted him to eat well, but he was a woodcarver and woodcarvers just didn't eat vegetables.

Zac put down his tools as Ana placed the plate on his workbench. He liked eating his midday meal in the workshop, and he liked how she talked with him as he ate. It seemed it was the only time she ever came to the workshop.

As Ana sat on one of the workshop stools, Zac took his first forkful of the delicious stew and spied the broccoli that she had hidden beneath the meal.

He pointed out the window at the chrysalis hanging from Yorah's branches, hoping to distract Ana long enough to feed the broccoli to Pook. "Ana, it looks like the doth could emerge any time now," he said.

"I see," she said with a smile, knowing full well what he was trying to do. She leaned out the window, pretending to look at the chrysalis, to give Zac time to throw away the vegetables.

Zac held the broccoli in front of chubby Pook who would eat just about anything.

Pook, always ready for food, quickly rolled over and stood, hoping to get some of the stew. He gave the proffered broccoli a few sniffs and passed.

Zac tucked the broccoli back under his unfinished meal.

"Have you thought of a name?" Ana asked, turning to him.

"No, not really," Zac replied. "I thought we should wait and see what it's like. You know, like Pook, who—"

"Yes, I know how Pook got his name," she interrupted, rolling her eyes skyward.

As Zac finished the stew, he wondered how he would dispose of the broccoli. If he couldn't come up with a plan soon, he would have to eat it to please his bride.

Outside the workshop window, the doth wriggled within the chrysalis, slowly at first, but soon it began moving vigorously, coiling within its home.

Pook backed himself onto one of Zac's boots and tried pulling his head into his body like a turtle. He wanted to hide. Even if everyone else was looking forward to the new doth, he wasn't. He could ignore the fairies but not a new doth. It would be just someone else to get his table scraps and eat his purple thistles. Worst of all, it was someone to come between him and Zac. This was not what he wanted.

"Look!" Zac cried. "The new doth is emerging!" He and Ana rushed to the window to watch.

The wet creature pushed out of its cocoon, teetered on a branch outside the workshop window, and flapped its wings dry.

"Isn't he cute?" asked Ana. "He's so sweet. Look at his big brown eyes. I could just kiss him."

As she reached out the workshop window to pet him, he suddenly and powerfully spread his wings and soared in through the window past her.

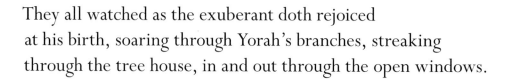

"Oh, dear!" exclaimed Ana, startled.

They all watched as the exuberant doth rejoiced at his birth, soaring through Yorah's branches, streaking through the tree house, in and out through the open windows.

"Oh," said Ana again. "He's so powerful and reckless—so energetic."

"Wow!" yelled Zac, jumping off his workbench seat, knocking Pook to the floor. "How great is this? A really powerful doth—I'll never have to worry about tam-o'jacks or grubinmoles again. And he can keep pace with me while I'm walking in the forest. He'll shoo away the fairies. Fantastic!"

Pook lowered his head and sat on the floor where he had fallen from Zac's boot. He already had been forgotten. He wasn't needed.

Ana ducked as the new doth made another pass through the room, buzzing over her head.

Pook hid under the workbench and closed his eyes.

"Look at him go," cheered Zac, jumping up and down.

The doth made another buzz in through the window, spun around, changed his direction to go back out the window but recklessly smashed into the wall of tools hanging beside Zac's workbench. Tools flew from the wall and crashed to the floor.

Without stopping, the doth quickly composed himself and soared back out the window.

Zac sat back on his stool and slapped his knees in amazement. "What a powerful doth! This is amazing! What should we call him?" he asked, furrowing his brow. "Maybe we should call him something that relates to recklessness? How about Wrecks Less? You know, Rex Less? Or, maybe just Rex?"

The doth sped back in through the window and slid to a stop in the middle of the fallen tools, noisily scattering them further.

"Wrecks Less?" asked the slightly annoyed Ana. "How about Wrecks More? Whatever it is, he should be named after one of his features."

"I'm thinking," Zac said, ignoring her suggestion, tapping his forehead with his index finger while looking at the new doth who excitedly wagged his tail and licked his nose.

As Zac pondered a new name, the overeager doth plopped himself at Zac's feet, lowered his front end, raised his back end, drooled, snorted, licked his obviously runny nose, wagged his tail, and gave a playful *grr*.

"Oh no, Zac! His nose runs," Ana said in disgust. "Well, at least he's not shy," she added. "He doesn't seem to be afraid of anything. He's definitely not like our chubby Pook."

Pook slid further under the workbench.

Zac smiled as an idea for the new doth's name started to form. "Let's see how confident he really is," he said, leaning down and putting his face close to the seated, energetic, brown doth's nose. "Boo," Zac said playfully.

Unexpectedly, the excited doth reacted with glee—like it was playtime. He spun three times in place, spread his powerful wings, zoomed out one window, zoomed in another, and plopped himself at Zac's feet and again responded with a friendly *grr*.

Zac and the doth played the game again and again, each time starting with a *boo* and ending with a *grr*.

Finally, Zac stopped the game and clapped his hands together. He had thought of the perfect name.

From his wry expression, Ana could tell he had picked a name and she couldn't resist reading his thoughts. It was worse than she expected.

"Oh no, Zac," she pleaded. "You can't call him that."

Chapter 9
The Name

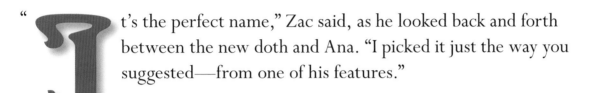

"**I**t's the perfect name," Zac said, as he looked back and forth between the new doth and Ana. "I picked it just the way you suggested—from one of his features."

Ana crossed her arms over her chest and stared at Zac disapprovingly.

"What?" he asked. "It's perfect. I just combined what I said and what he said."

Annoyed, she tapped her foot on the floor.

"And he licks his nose," he added, smiling, trying to justify his selection and win her over. "*Boo* and *grr*—it makes the perfect name. Just put the words together and you get . . . Booger!"

"Oh, Zac, we can't call him boo . . . boo . . . boog . . . ," she stammered, unable to bring herself to say it. But finally she couldn't resist a smile. The name was perfect and funny, even if it was a little disgusting.

"He's probably hungry too," Zac said, realizing he might finally get rid of the vegetables. "He can have my delicious broccoli."

Zac held a forkful in front of the now seated doth who turned up his runny nose, refusing the offer emphatically by licking his nose with a broad swipe of his tongue—*ka-slurp*.

"Well, at least now we know the difference between broccoli and boogers," he said with a grin.

Ana wrinkled her nose. "What's that?"

"Doths won't eat broccoli."

Chapter 10
The Three Syzygies

fter Zac had finished his lunch, Ana took his plate, with the broccoli still on it, back to the kitchen.

She set it on the sunny counter, wondering what other recipe she could use to hide the vegetables. Suddenly the room grew dim.

"That's odd," she said to Yorah as she put down the plate. "It's getting dark and there's not a cloud in the sky."

Yorah stared up. "Oh, dear!" she gasped. "It's an eclipse of the sun—that's why it's getting dark at noon! This could be the time of the three syzygies."

"Siz-a-whats?" inquired Ana.

"*Siz-a-gees*," Yorah pronounced slowly. "A syzygy is an alignment of heavenly bodies, in this case, the sun, moon, and Earth. That's why eclipses occur: when the moon comes between the Earth and the sun, it blocks the sunlight—that's a solar eclipse—and the day turns dark until the moon continues on its orbit."

"Yes," agreed Ana, "I can see it happening."

"When the Earth comes between the moon and the sun," continued Yorah, "Earth's shadow falls over the moon, causing a lunar eclipse, and the moon turns dark and seems to disappear.

"Tonight," the wise tree told her, "the moon may go dark."

Now Ana's expression frightened Yorah.

"Oh no, dear, it's far from certain. If it's just one eclipse—even two—it's nothing to worry about. But if this is the time of the three, then the Great Forest and all its inhabitants—especially the Good Fairies—are in dire trouble," she warned.

"Trouble?" Ana repeated. "What kind of trouble could be brought by eclipses? They're so far away."

"Perhaps none," Yorah agreed. "But if it is the foretold event, then three terrible perils are predicted."

Ana felt a chill. "Three things?"

"Yes, these three things will be the result of three powerful spells—the Eclipse Spells—that can only be cast during each of a trio of syzygies."

"You mean spells cast by the Dark Fairies?" Even though Ana recalled that they had been banished to a cave at the edge of the forest, she shivered still harder as the room continued to darken, the moon creeping further across the face of the sun.

"Yes, sweetie, the Dark Fairies will cast the spells, I'm afraid so. Legend has it that if three eclipses occur on consecutive days and nights, a new Darkling leader will emerge and use the *Book of Dark Spells* to kill all the Good Fairies."

Ana drew a sharp breath. "Kill the fairies? Why?"

"For their rings," Yorah explained sadly. "For the Fairy Rings of Eternal Life around their necks."

"Oh," Ana gasped. She had forgotten all about the rings and their ugly history. "Yes, now I remember, Yorah," she said at last, recalling the ancient lore about the Hest, ancestors to all elves and fairies, good and evil. "The Hest's gift of the rings to all the fairies allowed them to stay young, to live forever."

"That's right," said Yorah. "The Hest created the rings using the *Book of Light Spells*. Every fairy got a ring, but then some fairies turned evil, and became Darklings. As punishment, the Hest took their rings back. That's when the Darklings stole the book and turned it into the *Book of Dark Spells* to help them do more evil."

"Where is the book now?" Ana asked.

"No one's seen it in years," answered Yorah. "It was probably kept by one of the Malic Hest, the smartest of the Hest's most evil descendents."

"How did they change it?"

"According to legend, the Malic Hest fancied themselves alchemists. They first modified the book just to make new Rings of Eternal Life, but they weren't smart enough to read the ancient Hest language. Yet they were able to change the book enough to create at least three new powerful Eclipse Spells."

As Yorah explained, Ana watched the line of dimness advance across a once bright patch of grass beyond her window.

"No one knows the first two Eclipse Spells," Yorah continued, "but the third is the Eclipse Spell of Good Fairies Death and it is meant to kill all the Good Fairies."

"So that is how the Darklings will get the rings?" Ana whispered.

"That's right," said Yorah. "The Dark Fairies want the Good Fairies' rings and they will kill to get them."

As Yorah finished, the noonday sun was disappearing in a cloudless sky—the sun, moon, and Earth almost perfectly aligned.

Chapter 11

The Second Eclipse

ar also watched the darkening day as the second eclipse approached. As the day got gloomier, he stood at the mouth of the cave and began his second spell, reading the page from the upper left, turning the book as he chanted.

"Growth anew, I command you," he screamed, looking skyward. As did all the spells in the book, the Eclipse Spell took its toll on the one who spoke it: Dar's skin erupted with gray, fuzzy growths.

"Become now past."

He waited, knowing the last line of the spell needed to be cast at the peak of the eclipse.

He watched the moon as it covered the sun, the bright day becoming as dark as night. Then he read the final line: "This spell I cast."

More growths appeared on his skin, covering him with gray fuzz like a moldy peach. He didn't care; the second spell was now complete.

The food and crops throughout the Great Forest would become moldy, unfit to eat except by Darklings. The humans in the village would soon leave to find food, abandoning the Great Forest to the Dark Fairies, and preventing them from finding the Fairy Rings.

"Last spell tonight," Dar whispered. "Tonight spell last."

He wiped the mold from his arms and head and shuffled back into the cave to wait.

Chapter 12

The Mold

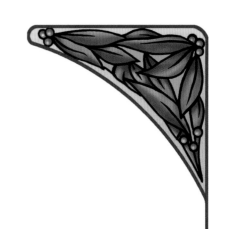

As the eclipse of the sun passed and the light once again shone in the forest, Ana left Yorah, crossed the swinging bridge and descended the circular staircase around the Great Oak. She walked down the short garden path, past the ivy-covered brick wall, and passed under the stone arch into the small orchard that Zac maintained so they could always have fresh fruit.

She stood on her toes, reached high above her head, and plucked one of the pippin apples for Zac's dessert.

The apple was covered with gray, fuzzy mold.

She threw it down and picked another, then another. All the apples had been struck by the mold, along with the fruit on the other trees.

She wiped the mold off her fingers and returned to the tree house empty-handed.

STADTHER KAMMERER '06

Chapter 13
Yorah

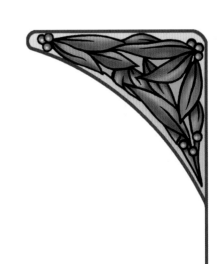

That afternoon in his workshop, Zac completed the tea box he was making, Ana sang with the Flower Fairies, Booger soared through Yorah's leaves, the Kootenstoopits rummaged through the dresser drawers looking for socks and buttons to steal, the Pickensrooters banged box lids, and Pook hid under the workbench.

By evening everyone was tired and ready for sleep.

While Yorah and the inhabitants of her branches slept—with Pook under the covers at the foot of the bed and the new doth on the floor near Zac—the breathless Forest Creatures, led by Ladybug, finally arrived at the Great Oak and perched themselves on the tip of Yorah's nose.

"Madame Oak! Wake up!" shouted Ladybug. "Wake up!"

"Wake up?" mumbled the sleepy, startled Yorah. "Uh . . . yes. Yes, dearie, of course I'm awake." Bleary eyed, Yorah struggled to focus on the group of Creatures assembled before her.

"Madame Oak!" yelled Ladybug, "Dragonfly saw a Dark Fairy last night reading from an old book."

"Well, well," chuckled Yorah in her sleepy haze, not remembering her conversation with Ana earlier that day about the *Book of Dark Spells*.

"Most Darklings can't read," Yorah muttered. "It's probably nothing to worry about. It's probably a book they stole from someone. I'm sure it means nothing. Settle yourselves into my branches and have a good night's sleep."

"Good, now we can get zzzome zzzleep," buzzed tired Bee.

"Does this mean we can't eat the Dark Fairy?" asked disappointed Spider.

"Don't . . . forget . . . to . . . ," began slow Snail.

"Begging your pardon, madame," said the militant Dragonfly, "but we could still form Flight Formation Delta and attack him from the air."

". . . tell . . . her . . . about . . . ," struggled Snail.

"We could tie him up," said Spider, hungrily, "and hang him up." She rolled her eight eyes skyward, thinking, "and keep him for a rainy day's feast."

"Feast! Let's have a late-night snack," added the Ant.

"Hush, all of you!" said Ladybug forcefully. "Let's do as the wise Oak asks, make ourselves comfortable, and go to sleep."

They all prepared for a night's rest after their long and seemingly unnecessary trip to Yorah. Caterpillar began to build his silk tent. Beetle rolled onto his back.

". . . the . . . moon . . . disappearing . . . last . . . night. Whew," said Snail, exhausted.

By the time Snail had finished speaking, all the other Forest Creatures had settled down to sleep for the evening.

"The moon disappeared last night?" Yorah asked seriously, realizing with alarm that the eclipse earlier that day was not a lone event but the second of the three eclipses predicted.

"Oh, my!" she said to the Forest Creatures. "This evil one can only be Dar, the last of the Malic Hest. If he's not stopped, the Good Fairies will die. We must get that book and stop him!"

That did it. This was the opportunity the militant Dragonfly had been looking for.

"Condition Red!" he shouted. "We are under attack! I am now in command. Form Flight Formation Delta and proceed to the Grotto. We will attack and confiscate the book. That is all!"

Before Yorah could stop them, the Forest Creatures had assembled and flown from her branches, off to the Grotto to get the *Book of Dark Spells* from the evil Darkling leader.

Chapter 14
Yorah's Plan

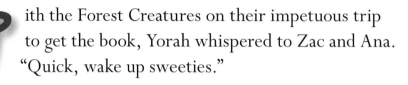ith the Forest Creatures on their impetuous trip to get the book, Yorah whispered to Zac and Ana. "Quick, wake up sweeties."

Booger bounded to his feet, letting out a series of bloodcurdling barks; Pook stayed under the covers in his nice warm spot at the foot of the bed, letting Booger handle the whatever-it-was that was making him bark.

Startled, Zac sat up.

"The third syzygy is approaching," Yorah said urgently. "The time we spoke about is here, Ana. The Good Fairies are about to die!"

"Syz-a-what?" asked the confused, sleepy Zac.

"Zac, we don't have time for words," Ana said, gasping, leaping out of bed. "You will have to listen to my thoughts."

Compelled by the urgency in his wife's voice, Zac listened to her thoughts. He now understood about the evil Dar, the three eclipses, and the three spells. He understood, too, the next spell would kill the Good Fairies.

"The third eclipse is tonight," warned Yorah. "You have to get the *Book of Dark Spells* and stop Dar from casting the spell to kill the Good Fairies."

Yorah called the Flower Fairies, Kootenstoopits, and Pickensrooters around her and quickly told them to fly to the Grotto and help the Forest Creatures take the book from Dar. Off they flew. The Flower Fairies led the way with the Pickensrooters carrying the slower Kootenstoopits.

"Zac, you and the doths will have to follow the fairies and stop Dar from casting the final spell," Yorah declared.

Zac grabbed his broad ax, instructed the two doths to follow, and headed to the Grotto to battle the evil Dar.

Chapter 15
The Crevasse

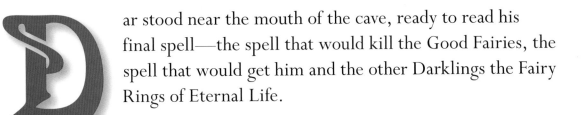

Dar stood near the mouth of the cave, ready to read his final spell—the spell that would kill the Good Fairies, the spell that would get him and the other Darklings the Fairy Rings of Eternal Life.

He watched the approaching eclipse with excitement from the limestone boulders outside the cave. His wings twitched as he looked into the night sky. He held the *Book of Dark Spells* open to the Eclipse Spell of Good Fairies Death, ready for his victory. Soon he would have the ring and he would never die.

He could see Zac and the two doths approaching far away down the mountain. A simple woodcarver and a couple of doths were not going to prevent him from casting his final spell. But he wasn't going to take any chances.

Dar turned to another spell in the book—the Chant Spell of Crevasse.

"Ground will shake and none can pass!" he yelled, glaring at Zac and the doths still far down the mountain.

Dar's
body shook
violently.

"This spell to
make a deep
crevasse," he
stuttered, finishing
the spell and falling
to the ground, his body
thrashing from the spell's
effect.

The ground shook and opened
near the mouth of the cave, too
wide for anyone to jump and too
long for anyone to walk around.
Dar was ready to continue his plan.

He hadn't counted on interference by
the flying Forest Creatures.

"Condition Red!" barked Dragonfly.
"Everyone charge!" he shouted to his fellow
Forest Creatures as the group arrived at
the Grotto where Dar stood.

Dragonfly, with Spider riding on his back, began the attack. He buzzed just under Dar's nose and banked around behind his head. Spider let fly with her web and lassoed Dar's neck as Dragonfly made several loops around the Dark Fairy.

Hummingbird flew directly at Dar's face. Grasshopper dropped on Dar's head, using his powerful legs to kick at his cranium while Hummingbird pecked at Dar's forehead.

"We've . . . got . . . him . . . ," said Snail.

Firefly, Beetle, and Caterpillar landed on the open book and began pulling at the pages, attempting to wrestle it from Dar's grasp.

Butterfly fluttered under Dar's nose, tickling him, while Ant stung him on the chin.

Ladybug hovered and shook her foreleg at the Darkling. "You should be ashamed of yourself!" she screamed.

To the Forest Creatures, the battle seemed to be going their way.

Snail was still speaking, mid-sentence, ". . . just where . . ."

Then Dar violently shook his body, flinging the Forest Creatures in all directions with flightless Snail, Ant, and Grasshopper falling toward the ground.

"Condition Red! Retreat to Flight Formation Delta!" yelled Dragonfly.

Dar, more annoyed by the puny assault than afraid, realized that the Forest Creatures would be preparing for another attack. Quickly he flipped the book's pages until he came to another spell—the Chant Spell of Descend.

The flying Creatures had all caught their crawling companions and regrouped for another attack.

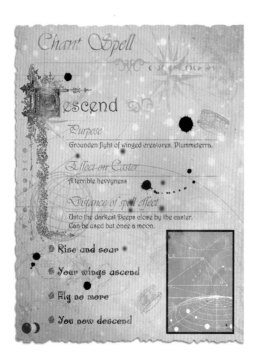

Dar gleefully looked at the small group flying around him and began the new spell. "Rise and soar, your wings ascend," he hissed maliciously.

The flying Forest Creatures began to rise higher into the sky. Dar's wings fluttered too and he momentarily rose from the ground from the effect of the spell's backlash.

"Fly no more, you now descend," he finished coldly.

Their wings, now motionless from Dar's spell, no longer supported the Forest Creatures and into the deep crevasse they fell.

Dar's wings drooped.

Snail completed his thought just as he and the other Creatures descended into the darkness, ". . . he . . . wants . . . us."

Chapter 16

The Rumbling Stopped

S till far down the mountain below the Grotto, Zac fell to his knees as Dar's spell shook the ground. Pook plopped onto his rear end. He closed his eyes, hoping not to see anything scary.

Booger, soaring on his powerful wings, instantly flew to Zac's side to be certain his master wasn't hurt.

"Good boy," Zac said. "Everything's all right. No one is hurt."

Booger excitedly flew into Zac's arms and gave him a big wet lick across his chin.

The rumbling stopped and Pook's eyes popped open. He could see the new doth was getting all Zac's attention again.

Chapter 17
The Good Fairies Attack

Dar glanced at the woodcarver and the doths, down the mountain. They were still too far away for him to worry about, especially since the crevasse was too wide for them to cross.

He focussed his attention on the swarm of Good Fairies that had just flown over the crevasse and now swirled around his head.

The normally silly Kootenstoopits pulled menacingly at Dar's shoestrings. The Flower Fairies hovered around his eyes, blocking his vision, and the agile Pickensrooters pulled at his clothes, tugged at his leggings, poked him in the nose, and wrestled with the *Book of Dark Spells*.

They confused and confounded him. As if being attacked by a hive of bees, he swatted and swiped at them, tormented, missing every time. Some even taunted him as if playing a game, laughing and giggling, tickling him. He was losing the battle.

As the fairies tickled and tugged, Dar spun around, nearly losing his balance, and the fairies pulled the book from his hands.

At the last second, Dar flapped his stubby wings enough to lurch upward and grab the vital page—the Eclipse Spell of Good Fairies Death. He tore the page from the book as the fairies flew off with the remainder.

"You have book. Book have you," Dar muttered. "I have spell. Spell have I. Soon Good Fairies die. Die Fairies Good soon."

Chapter 18
The Fairies Return

A na struggled to hear Zac's thoughts as he approached the crevasse that separated him from the evil Dar. She knew he was too far to hear her thoughts. Try as she might, she couldn't help him.

As she listened, the fairies arrived with the *Book of Dark Spells*.

Ana took the book from the fairies and held it for Yorah to see. They both read the cover.

Yorah said, "This is it—the *Book of Dark Spells*! If we can figure out its secrets, maybe we can reverse the spells cast by Dar and save the Good Fairies."

They paged through the book. Some parts were clear, others mysterious.

They read about the simple Chant Spells—the spells that could be cast easily by anyone just by reading the spell's words. They studied the mysterious Eclipse Spells that could only be cast during an eclipse. They wondered at the strange, incomplete Light Spells with their missing words and strange symbols.

Some of the mysterious symbols in the book seemed to make no sense whatsoever. The ancient Hest symbols, the maps, and the spells swirled in Ana's mind. The solution had to be right before her eyes.

"This book is the *Book of Light Spells*," Yorah reminded her, "but it has been changed by the Malic Hest so that it doesn't make any sense. The Malic Hest have even somehow changed the cover of the book to *Dark Spells Dark*."

"Well, we have to figure this out," said Ana. "It's the only way we can reverse the spells and save the Good Fairies."

They pored through the book, looking at its mysterious contents. The now reddening moon shone through the bedroom window, breaking their concentration.

"We have to hurry," said Ana. "The third eclipse is starting!"

Chapter 19
The Third Eclipse

ac and the doths reached the edge of the chasm as Dar, on the far side near the mouth of the cave, began his third spell—the Eclipse Spell of Good Fairies Death.

With the torn page in hand, his stubby wings twitching excitedly, Dar pointed at the darkening moon and began reading.

"It will you all replace!" he shouted, as he watched the approaching eclipse.

Without hesitation or instruction from Zac, Booger impetuously started over the crevasse, carried by his powerful wings. Pook hesitated, poised at the edge of the seemingly bottomless crack in the Earth, unsure if his tiny wings could carry his heavy body across.

Then, bravely and clumsily, Pook leaped, his legs and wings flapping in all directions. But try as he might, his brave efforts were not enough, and with his wings flapping as fast as he could, he sank lower and lower into the crevasse.

He wasn't going to make it.

Chapter 20
The Book of Light Spells

"**T**his book makes no sense," Ana said exasperatedly. "I don't see any way to reverse the spells that released the Darklings and caused the mold."

"The eclipse has begun! We have to hurry!" shouted Yorah, watching as the shadow of the Earth spread across the moon. "Concentrate, dearie," she urged. "Use your halfling senses to understand the book."

Ana closed her eyes and thought about the book's strange symbols. As all halflings were taught to do, she began to think of things differently—to see things that others didn't see—things that were not obvious but in plain sight. The strange symbols swirled in her mind.

Then, opening her eyes, she shouted, "I've got it! I know the book's secrets! I know how to read it!"

She turned the *Book of Dark Spells* upside down and held it up for Yorah to see.

"Look! Look at the title of the book. Upside down it's the *Book of Light Spells*." By turning the book, the title had magically changed from Dark Spells Dark to Light Spells Light. It had been right in front of her all the time.

With the book still upside down, she thumbed through its pages until she saw the Spell of Grow.

"Look," she said to Yorah. "Upside down, the mold spell now becomes the Eclipse Spell of Grow. Dar must have read it the other way, on the second eclipse, making everything moldy. Now, during this eclipse we can read it

the right way and make things grow again."

She then turned to the Eclipse Spell of Light Fairies Close. "This must be the spell that will put the Dark Fairies back into the cave. We have to read them together and just hope Zac prevents Dar from casting the Eclipse Spell of Good Fairies Death."

They began their spells together.

"Become now past," read Yorah.

"Take flight now leave," Ana said nervously.

As the moon reddened, the third and last syzygy fast approaching, the pair continued saying their spells.

"This spell I cast," Yorah said forcefully.

"And heed my call," said Ana.

The eclipse peak neared.

"Growth anew," said Yorah, speaking her penultimate line.

"Fairies in the cave," said Ana.

Before they had completed their spells, Ana suddenly sensed danger for Booger and Pook.

Chapter 21
Ana's Dream Was Right

ac fell to his knees and stared into the crevasse. "Pook!" he shouted, not knowing what to do for his friend as Pook disappeared into the crevasse's blackness.

On the other side, Dar continued his spell. "Fairies breath now begun!" he shouted, unconcerned the strong brown doth was headed right for him.

Zac watched as Booger lowered his head and flew toward Dar.

"Life yields to your embrace," Dar yelled as the powerful Booger plowed into him headfirst, sending him reeling, making him drop the spell page. It drifted in the night air and settled tantalizingly at the crevasse edge, where it teetered.

The Darkling coughed, caught his breath, and prepared for the next blow from the doth.

Booger backed up in flight, preparing to smash the evil fairy into the rocky cliff, then dived full speed at Dar.

But as Booger was about to collide with Dar, the evil fairy flapped his tiny wings enough to dodge the attack.

Booger smashed headfirst into the cliff wall and slumped to the ground, unconscious.

Stunned, Zac watched helplessly as Dar retrieved the spell page.

"You can't stop me now! Now me stop can't you!" he shouted across the crevasse at Zac.

The lunar eclipse was moments from its peak. Soon the Good Fairies would be dead, soon Dar and the Darklings would have their rings, and there was nothing anyone could do to stop it.

Dar looked again at the moon. The eclipse's peak had not passed. There was still time to complete his spell.

"And now it is . . . ," he screamed, almost finishing the last line of the spell.

As he was about to say the last word, he was thrown to the ground, upended by something yanking at his leggings.

"Pook!" Zac shouted.

The chubby and determined doth was not going to let the Good Fairies die. He had used all of his might to fly out of the deep crevasse. His powerful jaws locked onto Dar's leggings, his tiny wings flapping furiously as he pulled the evil one forward.

"Arrrgh!" the Darkling shouted, trying to shake the doth off his leg.

Pook held fast and inched Dar toward the crevasse.

Then, as Pook was about to pull him over the ledge, Dar's old leggings snapped. Pook, catapulted from the unleashed force, tumbled into the crevasse again. Dar stood with the spell in his hand, exhausted. It was now time. The eclipse was at its peak.

With his back to the cave, he cleared his throat and began the last spell line again.

"And now it is . . . ," he read energetically, pausing and preparing to shout the last word.

Then he screamed in pain as Booger smashed into his back, sending Dar and the spell tumbling into the crevasse.

At that moment, far away in the tree house, Ana and Yorah completed their spells.

"I command you," said Yorah, finishing the Eclipse Spell of Grow, eliminating the mold from the Great Forest.

"I command you all," shouted Ana, also completing her spell, spiriting the evil Dark Fairies helplessly back into their dark cave.

Zac knelt at the edge of the black crevasse. Pook had fallen almost out of sight. There was no way Pook could save himself now, and no way Zac could save his best friend from death.

Ana's dream had been right.

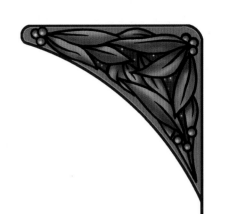

Chapter 22
Arise

Far away in the tree house, just as she had finished her spell, Ana could sense Pook falling. As in her dream, she feared Pook would die.

She frantically flipped the book's pages until she found the Chant Spell of Arise which she hoped would help Pook. She began saying the spell. "Fly and arise—"

Chapter 23

A Lighter Shadow in the Shadows

Booger wasn't going to let Pook die at the bottom of the hole created by the Darkling. He dove into the black crevasse as fast as his powerful wings would carry him, keeping a keen eye on Pook so he wouldn't lose him in the darkness.

Zac watched from the edge of the crevasse, waiting and staring into the dark hole. He knelt and leaned in, hoping to see or hear something.

He could hear only the blood pounding in his temples and the ragged sound of his heavy breathing.

From deep in the crevasse, he heard a whisper, almost imagined. He held his breath. He heard a soft whoosh. Then another.

Finally the whoosh changed to flapping and then to the familiar flutter of doth wings.

It was Booger lifting Pook out of the crevasse, pulling him up, holding Pook's tiny wings in his powerful jaws.

Zac jumped, cheering. "Hooray!" He could see the doths clearly now rising toward him.

Pook's rescue was almost complete, but just as Booger lifted Pook over the edge, one of Pook's hind feet got stuck on a root protruding from the crevasse wall.

Zac lay at the edge of the crevasse, reaching for Pook. Zac reached as far as he could. Booger flapped his wings harder, stretching the stuck doth. Booger tugged harder and harder. Zac leaned farther into the crevasse.

Without warning, Pook's tiny wings, pulled beyond their limit, tore from his body.

The force unleashed from Pook's breaking wings shot Booger skyward and sent Pook plummeting into the crevasse's shadows.

Back at the tree house, Ana completed the Spell of Arise. "Spell I utter. Into the skies, wings aflutter."

Chapter 24

It Would Be Like Old Times

Zac sank to his knees. "Why, Pook?" he asked as if Pook could hear him. "Why were you so brave today? Booger could have stopped Dar. You didn't have to die."

Zac and Booger turned and began their sad trip back to the tree house, satisfied that the Great Forest was back to normal and pleased Dar's spells had been reversed. They had saved the Good Fairies.

Before they walked a few steps from the crevasse, they heard a commotion behind them, and then a flapping of very tiny wings.

Aided by Ana's last spell, the twelve Forest Creatures tugged and strained as they lifted the heavy Pook out of the hole with Spider's web. The happy and very much alive little doth held the spell page torn from the book in his mouth.

"Pook!" shouted Zac.

Pook leaped from the web and landed hard in Zac's arms, knocking the wind out of him. Pook leaned his head back and smiled broadly.

All was perfect in the Great Forest. When they got back to their tree house, it would be like old times.

Chapter 25

Where Are the Good Fairies?

As they headed back to the tree house, the sun rose over the peaceful forest. Zac merrily whistled one of the nonsense fairy songs as he walked the path back to his home, knowing he would soon be with Ana. It was a beautiful morning, made even more

beautiful
because they
had saved the
Good Fairies.

Pook walked at his usual pokey pace behind Zac
with Booger flying ahead.

"Hooray!" Zac shouted. "We saved the fairies!
I can't wait to tell Ana how you both worked
together to stop the evil Darkling."

When they arrived at the
normally bright

and cheerful tree house, it was quiet and dark, the windows shuttered. Something was wrong.

"Why is it so quiet?" Zac asked with trepidation. "Where are the fairies?"

He bounded up the circular stairs and crossed the swinging bridge to the center room, eager to see his wife. As he entered the dark room, he could faintly see Yorah's face, illuminated only by the light from the door he had not quite shut. Her eyes were closed.

She slowly opened them as he walked closer. Zac could see they were sad eyes—old eyes—filled with wisdom from hundreds of years of life, and they were eyes filled with tears.

Before Yorah could speak to explain her sorrow, Booger and Pook pushed into the room, opening the door fully, allowing more sunlight to enter, revealing Ana's body, collapsed on the floor.

Chapter 26
The Syzygies Are Over

ac rushed to his bride, fell to his knees, and held her in his arms. "Ana, speak to me! Speak to me!" he shouted frantically, shaking her.

"She can't hear you, Zac," sobbed Yorah, barely able to speak. "She's dead, Zac. Ana's dead."

"She can't be dead," howled Zac, hugging her body tightly.

"She was killed by the Eclipse Spell of Good Fairies Death with all the other Good Fairies," explained Yorah.

"The spell? What spell? Dar didn't finish the spell. I saw him fall into the crevasse before he could finish it."

"No, dear one, Dar wasn't stopped. Ana told me what was happening. He must have finished his spell as he fell."

"But why did Ana die? Dar meant his spell for the Good Fairies," Zac moaned.

"Zac," Yorah said gently, "long ago, Good Fairies and elves were closely related. Since Ana was part elf, she was also a tiny part Good Fairy, and when Dar cast his spell, she died with the other Good Fairies."

"But the two of you reversed the spells—didn't you? So, we can do it again. I . . . I . . . I'll get the book," he stammered.

"No, Zac. It's no use. It was an Eclipse Spell and the syzygies are over. There are no spells to bring her back to life. I'm sorry, but the spells can't be reversed," Yorah sobbed. "Ana is gone."

Chapter 27
The Celestial Dance

On the floor of the dimly lit room, Zac held his wife's body. Pook and Booger sat helplessly beside the couple.

High in Yorah's leaves, the Forest Creatures stared down at Zac holding Ana's lifeless body—for once, they were speechless. Dragonfly and Spider didn't have a reckless plan, Ladybug didn't take control, and Snail didn't struggle to speak.

Yorah, helpless too, silently wept and stared at the couple, realizing her best friend—the young halfling girl who she first met singing with the Flower Fairies in her branches—was gone, as were the fairies.

High above the tree house where Zac held Ana, the sun shone down onto the quiet forest. The Earth circled the sun as it always had and the moon continued its path around the Earth.

The celestial dance of the sun, moon, and Earth continued, but the syzygies were over.

Chapter 28

Life Yields to Your Embrace

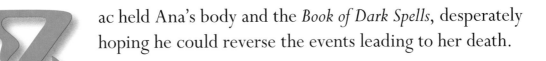ac held Ana's body and the *Book of Dark Spells*, desperately hoping he could reverse the events leading to her death.

He stared at the cover of the book and turned its pages. He wondered about the spells—the strange sun and moon symbols—and then he read the incomplete Light Spell of Reversi Luna.

"Can I still hear her thoughts?" he whispered. "Can she still somehow be alive?"

He knew she had figured out the secrets of the book. If only he could hear her thoughts now. But he hadn't tried listening to them enough over the last year, and even if she were alive, he probably couldn't hear her thoughts. Yet he refused to let her go.

He closed his eyes, cleared his thoughts, and waited.

Gradually he sensed something or someone talking to him—putting thoughts and images into his mind. He didn't know if it was Ana's thoughts he heard, but the secrets of the book slowly became clear, like a secret code being revealed. The symbols in the book swirled and coalesced in his mind, combined and formed anew, and gradually, he understood them.

All he had to do was reverse everything. But Yorah had told him there were no more eclipses. She said the syzygies were over. He needed another eclipse.

The thin shaft of sunlight coming through the door fell across the anniversary couple. Zac looked at his beautiful bride of two years, the light bathing her face, silhouetting her lovely halfling features. As he held her in the dim room she was still the most beautiful halfling girl in the world.

As he looked at the light that accentuated her beautiful face, the truth suddenly struck him. "Of course," he shouted. "Light! The secret is light!"

He turned to the incomplete Light Spell of Reversi Luna—reverse the moon! If he could complete the spell—find the missing words to the spell—he could create another eclipse and then use one of the other powerful Eclipse Spells to save Ana and the Good Fairies.

He stared at the page, ripped it from the book, and held it directly between him and the sun—a kind of syzygy—an alignment of the sun, the page, and Zac.

The spell's secret became clear as the light shone through the page, revealing the hidden message.

Zac began reading, "Lunar orb on your way around your circular equation."

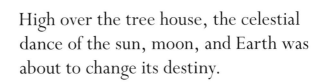

High over the tree house, the celestial dance of the sun, moon, and Earth was about to change its destiny.

Zac continued, "A celestial dance you must obey, and reverse your current motion."

The dance of the celestial spheres paused as the moon slowed and stopped from the effect of the powerful Light Spell. Then the moon slowly reversed its path back between the sun and the Earth—a new eclipse had begun and the bright day darkened.

Zac started the final part of his plan, taking the Eclipse Spell of Good Fairies Death page from Pook and turning it upside down, changing it into the Eclipse Spell of Good Fairies Life.

The day darkened more.

He read the spell on the opposite end of the page from where Dar had read it, "Life yields to your embrace and now it is done."

In the almost completely dark room, Zac held his wife in his arms as the eclipse peaked.

"It will you all replace fairies breath now begun," he shouted with hopeful anticipation.

After he said the words "fairies breath now begun," Zac heard a rush of air, like a large, communal breath being drawn. Countless Good Fairies were coming back to life.

He had completed the spell, but as the moon passed the sun and the day began to brighten, Ana lay still in his arms. The spell had not worked for her. He pressed his face to hers. He had failed. He hadn't listened to his wife's thoughts well enough.

As the day brightened more, Ana gasped a deep breath, arching her back, struggling. She was fighting to come back to life, to be back with Zac.

After several deep breaths, she opened her eyes, put her hand to his cheek and smiled weakly, knowing he had heard her dying thoughts and saved her life.

Chapter 29

The Anniversary

Ana was still unsteady as Zac held her but she remembered their anniversary and reached into the pocket of her dress and took out something, concealing it between her hands.

"Happy anniversary, darling," she said, placing the present into Zac's hand.

He stared at the gift—a tiny wooden box. Because of his struggle with Dar, he had forgotten today was their wedding anniversary.

"I hope you like it. I made it myself," she said shyly.

"H-h-how did you . . . w-w-when did you . . . ?" he stammered, examining and admiring the box.

"I watched how you make boxes and I made it in your workshop at night while you slept. It's not very good," she said.

He looked at her lovingly, now realizing that it was she and not the fairies who had rearranged his tools at night. "It's beautiful. It's the most beautiful box I've ever seen," he said. "Can I open it?"

He didn't wait to hear her answer and eagerly opened the box, revealing a clover blossom curled into a ring.

"I made you a clover blossom ring like the one you first gave me," she said sweetly.

She took the ring out of the box and placed it on his finger, just as he had done for her two years ago when he proposed under Yorah's branches.

Zac, beaming with pride, smiled and leaned to kiss his wife. He pulled her close and looked adoringly into her beautiful dark halfling eyes. He could feel her breath against his cheek. As he was about to kiss her, he remembered, drew back, and lowered his head, ashamed he had nothing to give her.

"I'm sorry," he said. "I don't have anything to give . . ." He stopped speaking before completing his thought, realizing he could give his wife something for their anniversary—now that he understood the secrets of the *Book of Spells*.

As Ana watched, he grabbed the book and turned to one of the spells for creating a ring. He concentrated on the symbols and recited the spell—reading the old Hest symbols easily now, as if it were a children's book.

Then he recited the spell to summon the ring.

When he was done, he held out his clenched hand. A bright red light briefly flickered within his closed fist, piercing the spaces between his fingers.

He opened his hand and in his palm lay the ring he had summoned with the spell, two bands of jewels with one red diamond between them—a Fairy Ring of Eternal Life.

Zac took his bride's hand and lovingly placed the new ring on her finger—knowing that by wearing it she would never get old, and she would never die.

"Happy anniversary," he said as he pulled her into his arms.

The Flower Fairies, Pickensrooters, and Kootenstoopits appeared, laughing and giggling, flying around the lovers—all the Good Fairies had come back to life from the spell cast by Zac.

In through the door flew Ladybug and Hummingbird with Grasshopper perched on his back. Ant rode in atop Butterfly, Bee held onto Snail, Spider onto Dragonfly, and the heavy Caterpillar was carried by Firefly and Beetle.

The Forest Creatures flew into Yorah's branches and watched the loving couple who sat staring into each other's eyes.

Dragonfly spoke first. "Whoa! It looks like we've got some serious mutual reconnaissance going on here."

"Look how close he is to her. He's going to devour her," said the delighted, bloodthirsty Spider.

Snail began speaking slowly, "He's . . . not . . . going . . ."

"Everybody, stay back," shouted Ladybug. "Leave them alone! They're in love."

". . . to . . . devour . . . her. . . ," Snail continued.

"Aren't they as sweet as nectar?" fluttered Butterfly.

". . . he's . . . going . . . ," Snail said slowly.

"Ain't she be-yoo-ty-ful," cracked Ant. "She's prettier than an open picnic basket!"

"Hush, all of you!" scolded Ladybug. "Leave them alone!"

Snail finished speaking with a sigh, ". . . to . . . kiss . . . her. *Whew.*"

Pook and Booger sat together on the floor eagerly watching the anniversary couple whose lips drew closer; the doths were perfectly poised to jump between the couple—destroying their moment. Pook gently barked *uff-uff.* Booger excitedly wagged his tail and licked his nose, scarcely restraining himself from jumping on the couple.

But as Zac and Ana drew close, the two doths stayed where they were, stared at the lovers, and watched their tender kiss.

The End

Appendix

The Rings

Extremely Rare "One of a Kind" Natural Fancy Red Diamond Ring

18 Karat Rose Gold Ring containing a .59 carat Radiant Cut Natural Fancy Red Diamond surmounted by fifty-two (52) natural fancy and fancy intense pink diamonds in an Aaron Basha "Double Decker" custom design with natural pink diamond-set flowers all totaling an additional .79 carats. The finished ring weighs 6.35 grams.

Rare "One of Three" Natural Fancy Intense Blue Diamond Rings

18 Karat White Gold Ring containing a .54 carat Oval Brilliant Cut Natural Fancy Intense Blue Diamond surmounted by fifty-two (52) natural light to fancy blue diamonds in an Aaron Basha "Double Decker" custom design with natural blue diamond-set flowers all totaling an additional .82 carats. The finished ring weighs 7.18 grams.

Important "One of Four" Natural Fancy Vivid Yellow Diamond Rings

18 Karat Yellow Gold Ring containing a 1.01 carat Shield Mixed Cut Fancy Vivid Yellow Diamond and further articulated with thirty-eight (38) round full cut natural fancy vivid yellow diamonds–in an Aaron Basha "Double Decker" custom design with natural fancy vivid yellow diamond-set flowers all totaling an additional .72 carats. The finished ring weighs 6.80 grams.

Unique "One of Five" Natural Pink Diamond Rings

18 Karat Rose Gold Ring containing forty-six (46) light pink to fancy intense pink diamonds comprising three diamond set flowers nestled between the Aaron Basha "Double Decker" custom design totaling .93 carats. The finished ring weighs 5.62 grams.

Fanciful "One of Eighty-Seven" Enameled Ladybug Diamond Rings

18 Karat Yellow Gold, Green and Black Enameled Ladybug, and natural fancy intense yellow diamond-set flowers nestled between the near-colorless diamond-set shanks of this Aaron Basha "Double Decker" custom design ring totaling .75 carats. The finished ring weighs 6.39 grams.

NOTE: The total *Secrets of the Alchemist Dar* collection of one hundred Rare and Unique Fancy Color Diamond Rings are original, copyrighted designs of Aaron Basha of New York City. They were commissioned and adapted by Treasure Trove, Inc. with specific features, uses of gold alloys and rare colored diamonds, and thus are protected by limited edition rights inured to Treasure Trove, Inc.

Aaron Basha

Aaron Basha is known for his collection of magical treasures and masterful designs of 18 karat gold, gemstones, and colored enamel. His name is internationally recognized for the signature jeweled Baby Shoes, Love Bugs, spectacular diamond designs, and a high profile celebrity clientele.

Aaron Basha has an extraordinary family history dating as far back as 1906. Son to a mother who served as a jewel merchant to Middle Eastern royals and a father who prospered as a pearl dealer, Aaron traveled often. Inspired by his excursions through the Persian Gulf cities and India, he acquired a love of rare jewels very early on. It was in 1959 that Aaron first began designing his own pieces and has since established himself as a Madison Avenue magnate and industry leader. Today, with the help of his wife and four children, Aaron Basha continues to delight the world with his whimsical charms and ever-expanding fine jewelry collection.

Aaron Basha boutiques can be found at renowned retailers worldwide in New York and London, as well as cities in Russia, Japan, Hong Kong, the Middle East, Europe, Latin America, and the Caribbean Islands.

"We are thrilled to be a part of the adventure of *Secrets of the Alchemist Dar*," says Aaron. "Our designs are known to charm the child at heart; may the Fairy Rings of Eternal Life bring fun, play, and love to all!"

For more information please visit www.aaronbasha.com

Acknowledgements

Treasure Trove, Inc. thanks the following:

Aaron Basha
680 Fifth Avenue
New York, New York 10021

Donald A. Palmieri, GG, ASA
Master Gemologist Appraiser®
580 Fifth Avenue
New York, New York 10036

Barry Lawrence Ruderman
Antique Maps Inc.
1298 Prospect, Suite 2C
La Jolla, California 92037
blr@raremaps.com

Appraiser's Note: May 2006

Michael Stadther has created an incredible global treasure hunt with some of the rarest earth treasures as the bounty. Of all the minerals that can be called precious gems, diamonds are surely king. The rarest of these magnificent gems, known for their incomparable brilliance, peerless durability, universal appeal, and extraordinary rarity are, of course, natural fancy color diamonds.

It is fitting that the author insisted the top treasure had to be the rarest of all rare earth diamonds—*a Fancy Red*. This remarkable treasure could not be an orangy red or a purplish red, which are typical modifiers of the red hue. It had to be a *"fancy red diamond"* without any modifiers. The search for such a stone covered four continents and was a treasure hunt, of sorts, in itself. Of the one hundred fancy color diamond rings, there is only one red diamond ring and it is valued for replacement at US$1,000,000.

In addition to this extremely rare red diamond, the ring created by the House of Aaron Basha is surmounted with fifty-two (52) *fancy to fancy intense pink diamonds*. This ring is truly one of a kind—protected by copyright and a special license granted to Treasure Trove, Inc. that limits production in order to create this extraordinary collection of one hundred *Secrets of the Alchemist Dar* Fancy Color Diamond Rings.

There are three second prize treasures, and they contain exceptionally rare *Fancy Intense Blue Diamonds*. It took many months to find the blue diamonds that illuminate the centerpiece of these treasures. Rare in nature, the blue diamond is the second rarest hue of fancy color diamonds. Once again, the 18 Karat white gold Aaron Basha ring is surmounted with *natural blue diamonds*. Each of these is valued at a retail replacement of US$120,000.

In his attempt to provide even more treasure hunters that extra incentive to solve the clues and find the treasures, the author commissioned the acquisition of four rare *Fancy Vivid Yellow Diamonds* to grace the centers of four Aaron Basha "Double Decker" rings surmounted with *fancy vivid yellow diamonds*. The retail replacement value of each is US$50,000.

There are five rose gold and pink diamond rings in the fourth category with three flowers strategically added for balance and grace—each delicate petal, a pink diamond, with a larger pink diamond in the center. Valued at retail replacement of US$20,000 each.

The remaining eighty-seven "Double Decker" rings represent the traditional Aaron Basha style with these yellow gold rings containing colorless diamonds along with two flowers set with intense yellow diamonds. These "Double Decker" rings are topped with one of the famous Basha green and black enameled ladybugs centered on each ring. Each of these quaint treasures is valued at US$5,500.

By commissioning Aaron Basha Design and Motif, the author has assembled a universally desirable and individually unique collection of rare and fanciful jeweled rings.

In all, treasure hunters are seeking over US$2,000,000 of rare diamond treasures.

If you need a little extra incentive to understand the value of the red diamond, there are approximately 155 carats to a troy ounce (31 grams). It would take approximately 262 of the fancy red diamonds like the first prize to equal a troy ounce, and, at the current value, that would be worth more than a quarter of a billion dollars (US). Of course, in all the current worldwide production, we don't think anyone could find 262 natural pure fancy red diamonds of this size, rare color, and exceptional clarity.

Once again, I am honored to have the opportunity to work on such a unique and challenging project. This incomparable collection will eventually be disbursed to all the successful treasure hunters throughout the world. Your families will share a bond that will transcend the boundaries of language, customs, geographical regions, and borders.

I wish you all good luck and good fortune!

All jewels were appraised by:
Gemological Appraisal Association, Inc. – NYC

Donald A. Palmieri, GG, ASA
Master Gemologist Appraiser®
President

All diamonds were certified and graded by:
Gem Certification & Assurance Lab, Inc. – GCAL – NYC
a division of Collectors Universe, Inc. (CLCT – NASDAQ)

Official Rules

A TREASURE'S TROVE: *Secrets of the Alchemist Dar*
Treasure Hunt Contest of Skill
Official Rules

1. HOW TO PARTICIPATE IN THIS PROMOTION (the "Treasure Hunt"): Obtain a copy of the book A Treasure's Trove: Secrets of the Alchemist Dar by Michael Stadther (the "Book"). Go to www.alchemistdar.com to register to play. Contained within the Book are puzzles and clues for you to solve. If you believe you have solved one of the puzzles, you will know how to redeem your ring (redemption instructions are part of the puzzle). Puzzles and clues can be solved by using your intellect and skill (chance plays no part in this Treasure Hunt). If you solve a puzzle, and you satisfy the eligibility requirements, follow the redemption instructions and you will, upon verification, receive the ring indicated. You must submit the claim personally; submissions through agents or third parties are not valid. The Book was first available to the public on September 26/27, 2006. The Treasure Hunt will run until all puzzles are solved and winners verified, or until December 30/31, 2009 (the "End Date"), whichever is sooner.

2. ELIGIBILITY: Open to legal residents of the 50 United States, including the District of Columbia, (except residents of the states of MD, ND and VT); the United Kingdom; Canada (void in Quebec); Ireland; Australia; New Zealand; France; Germany; Singapore, Hong Kong, and Japan. Pursuant to Japanese law, winners in Japan are subject to a different prize structure, as indicated below. Note that anyone may obtain the Book and participate by trying to solve the puzzles, but due to legal restrictions and the costs associated with obtaining legal clearance, only people residing in these jurisdictions may receive rings. Winners may be required to execute an affidavit swearing to compliance with these eligibility requirements. Employees of Sponsor, their immediate family and household members (related or not), and agents participating in the creation of this Treasure Hunt, are not eligible to enter.

3. DETAILS: Solutions to all puzzles in the Book have been recorded and are maintained in a secure location. Solutions will be revealed after the End Date, either on the web site or in a subsequent publication. You can learn more about the Book and the Treasure Hunt by going to the web site at www.alchemistdar.com.

4. PARTICIPANT CONDUCT: Sponsor reserves the right, in its sole discretion, to disqualify any Participant who (a) tampers with the entry process or the participation in, or operation of, the Treasure Hunt; (b) violates these rules; or (c) acts in a disruptive manner with the intent to annoy, abuse, threaten, or harass any other Participant or person. By participating, you agree to be bound by these Official Rules and the decisions of Sponsor, which shall be final in all respects on all aspects pertaining to the Treasure Hunt. Sponsor shall have complete discretion to interpret these Official Rules and any other aspect of the Treasure Hunt, and expressly reserves the right to refuse to award the ring to anyone who in Sponsor's discretion is in breach of these Official Rules or otherwise fails satisfactorily to establish their eligibility to win.

5. REDEMPTION INSTRUCTIONS: In order to receive your ring, YOU MUST KEEP YOUR SOLUTIONS TO THE PUZZLES CONFIDENTIAL. You may not share any solutions, or Sponsor may modify, terminate or suspend the Treasure Hunt, as described below. You will be asked to provide your solution(s) to the puzzles, and execute an affidavit of eligibility and liability/publicity release (where legal). If your responses are verified as accurate, and it is determined that you used your intellect and skill in order to solve a puzzle in the Treasure Hunt, provided you are in all other respects eligible to receive a ring, you will be declared a finder. Additional verification requirements and redemption instructions may be required. Winners must return the affidavit of eligibility and liability/publicity release within twenty–one (21) days of first attempted notification of verification. If Sponsor so elects, a potential prize winner may be required to submit to, and cooperate in, a confidential background check to confirm eligibility and to help ensure that the use of any such person in advertising or publicity for the Game will not bring Sponsor into public disrepute, contempt, scandal, or ridicule, or reflect unfavorably on the Game or the Sponsor as determined by Sponsor in its sole discretion. For winners who are younger than the age of majority, ring will be awarded in the finder's name to his/her parent or legal guardian, and affidavits and releases must be signed by the finder's parent or legal guardian. Winners must give Sponsor permission to publicize finder's name and hometown as a condition of receiving the ring, unless prohibited by law. Winners may also be required to use their names and submissions in advertising and marketing materials in all media in perpetuity, and may be required to participate in publicity events, except where prohibited by law. Sponsor reserves the right not to confirm verification of winners until after End Date.

6. COLLABORATIONS: If you have collaborated in your efforts with other persons, each of the participants must comply with all of the foregoing requirements and execute all of the required documents. Collaborators must also release Sponsor from any liability in connection with their agreement among one another, and if Sponsor incurs any costs or expenses, including legal expenses, in connection with collaborators' agreement, all collaborators agree to reimburse Sponsor for any and all such costs and expenses jointly and severally.

7. RINGS: 100 rings (except for Japan) will be available in the Treasure Hunt, with the following values:

	Appraised Value	Cash Substitution
1 @	US$1,000,000	US$300,000
3 @	US$120,000	US$40,000
4 @	US$50,000	US$15,000
5 @	US$20,000	US$6,000
87 @	US$5,500	US$1,650

A WINNING HOUSEHOLD MAY ONLY RECEIVE ONE RING PER RING LEVEL (TOTAL OF FIVE RINGS MAXIMUM, ONE FROM EACH LEVEL). Rings to be awarded include rings pictured as well as rings that may not be identical to rings pictured. All rings to be awarded will have appraised values equal to or greater than stated appraised values. Winners may elect to receive instead of the ring the cash substitution value listed above. All federal, state, provincial, and local taxes associated with the receipt or use of any ring and participation in the Treasure Hunt are the sole responsibility of the finder. It is the policy of the Sponsor, in compliance with United States Internal Revenue Service regulations, to send a Form 1099 to any US based winner receiving a ring valued in excess of $600 (USD), which requires disclosure of the winner's social security number. The winner remains solely responsible for paying all federal and other taxes in accordance with the laws that apply in your state of residence. If required by law, Sponsor reserves the right to withhold and remit to the appropriate taxing authorities the amount of any tax or taxes due. With respect to winners who accept the ring and not the cash substitution, it may be legally necessary under the United States Internal Revenue Code (as determined by Sponsor in its sole discretion) for the prize winner to pay the amount of any tax before receiving the prize. For winners outside the United States – United States tax law requires the payment of 30% (percent) of the value of the ring received as tax to the United States Internal Revenue Service. You will be asked to provide Sponsor with this tax payment prior to receiving your ring. In accordance with Japanese law, Japanese winners will not receive the prizes indicated above, but will receive prizes valued at the lesser of (a) 100,000 Yen or (b) the retail price of the book multiplied by twenty. Further, prizes offered to all Japanese winners will be capped at a maximum of two percent of the gross Japanese sales of the book.

8. GENERAL: All materials and submissions to Sponsor become property of the Sponsor and will not be returned. Sponsor accepts no liability for submissions, correspondence or attempted redemptions that are late, lost, or otherwise misdirected, or not submitted in accordance with these Official Rules. No transfer or substitution of rings permitted by winners, except as indicated herein.

9. ADDITIONAL LIMITATIONS: By entering, participants (a) agree to be bound by the Official Rules and the decisions of the Sponsor which are final and binding in all respects; (b) agree to release Sponsor and agents from any and all liability, loss, damage, or injury resulting from participation in this Treasure Hunt, as well as awarding, receipt, possession, use and/or misuse of any ring awarded herein and acknowledge that Sponsor, and agents have neither made nor are in any manner responsible or liable (to the extent permitted by law) for any warranty, representation, or guarantee, express, or implied, in fact or in law, relative to any ring including, but not limited to, its quality, mechanical condition, or fitness for a particular purpose; and (c) consent to use of his/her name, photograph and/or likeness for advertising and promotional purposes without additional compensation, unless prohibited by law. If one provision in these Official Rules is declared to be invalid for any reason, the balance of the Official Rules shall remain in full force and effect. If Sponsor so elects, a potential prize winner may be required to submit to, and cooperate in, a confidential background check to confirm eligibility and to help ensure that the use of any such person in advertising or publicity for the Game will not bring Sponsor into public disrepute, contempt, scandal, or ridicule or reflect unfavorably on the Game or the Sponsor as determined by Sponsor in its sole discretion.

10. DISPUTES: This Contest is governed by the laws of the United States and the State of New York, without respect to conflict of law doctrines. As a condition of participating in this Contest, participants agree that any and all disputes which cannot be resolved between the parties, and causes of action arising out of or in connection with this Contest, shall be resolved individually, without resort to any form of class action, exclusively before a court located in New York County, New York having jurisdiction. Further, in any such dispute, under no circumstances will participants be permitted to obtain awards for, and hereby waive all rights to claim punitive, incidental or consequential damages, including attorneys' fees, other than participant's actual out-of-pocket expenses (e.g. costs associated with entering), and participant further waives all rights to have damages multiplied or increased.

11. MOFIDICATION OR TERMINATION: Sponsor reserves the right, in its sole discretion, to modify, suspend, or terminate the Contest, and/or not award a specific ring, in the event solutions are published or otherwise shared; or should a virus, bugs or other causes beyond the control of the Sponsor corrupt the administration, security, or proper play of the contest. Sponsor is not responsible for late, lost, incomplete, or misdirected entries; computer system, phone line, equipment or program malfunctions, or other errors; failures or delays in computer transmissions or network connections; problems downloading anything from the web site; damage to entrant's or any other person's computer related to or resulting from participation or downloading any materials; or for any other technical problems related to entries.

12. PUBLICATION OF WINNERS: After the End Date of the Treasure Hunt, the winners will be published on the website.

13. SPONSOR: The Sponsor of this Treasure Hunt is Treasure Trove, Inc., 161 Cherry Street, New Canaan, CT 06840.

A TREASURE'S TROVE: les secrets de Dar l'alchimiste – Règlement officiel du Concours d'habileté Chasse au trésor

1. COMMENT PARTICIPER À CETTE PROMOTION (la « Chasse au trésor »): procurez-vous une copie du livre A Treasure's Trove : Les secrets de Dar l'alchimiste de Michael Stadther (le « livre »). Rendez-vous à l'adresse Web : www.alchemistdar.com pour vous inscrire au concours. Le livre contient des puzzles et des indices que vous devez résoudre. Si vous pensez avoir résolu un des puzzles, vous saurez comment échanger votre bague (les instructions pour l'échanger font partie du puzzle). Vous pouvez résoudre les puzzles et les indices en utilisant votre intelligence et votre habilité (la chance ne joue aucun rôle dans cette chasse au trésor). Si vous résolvez un puzzle et que vous répondez aux conditions de participation, suivez les instructions relatives à l'obtention de la bague et, après vérification, vous recevrez la bague indiquée. Vous devez soumettre la demande personnellement ; les demandes par l'intermédiaire de représentants ou de tiers ne sont pas valables. Le livre a été mis à la disposition du public pour la première fois les 26/27 septembre 2006. La chasse au trésor durera jusqu'à ce que tous les puzzles soient résolus et les gagnants confirmés ou jusqu'aux 30/31 décembre 2009 (la « date de clôture »), le premier événement survenant prévalant.

2. CONDITIONS DE PARTICIPATION: le concours est ouvert aux résidents légaux des 50 États Unis, y compris le District fédéral de Columbia (à l'exception des résidents des états du Maryland, du Dakota du Nord et du Vermont) ; le Royaume-Uni ; le Canada (interdit au Québec) ; l'Irlande; l'Australie, la Nouvelle-Zélande ; la France ; l'Allemagne ; Singapour ; Hong-Kong et le Japon. D'après la loi japonaise, les gagnants au Japon sont soumis à une structure de prix différente, telle qu'indiquée ci-après. Notez que quiconque peut se procurer le livre et participer au concours en essayant de résoudre les puzzles, mais à cause de restrictions légales et des coûts associés à l'obtention d'autorisations légales, seules les personnes résidant dans ces juridictions peuvent recevoir des bagues. Les gagnants peuvent avoir à faire une déclaration sous serment dans laquelle ils jurent qu'ils répondent à ces conditions de participation. Les employés du sponsor, leur famille proche et les personnes résidant à leur domicile (apparentées ou non), ainsi que les représentants participant à la création de cette chasse au trésor n'ont pas le droit de s'inscrire au concours.

3. DÉTAILS : les solutions à tous les puzzles du livre ont été enregistrées et sont conservées dans un endroit sûr. Les solutions seront révélées après la date de clôture, soit sur le site Web, soit dans une publication ultérieure. Vous pouvez en apprendre plus sur le livre et la chasse au trésor en vous rendant au site Web à l'adresse : www.thealchemistdar.com.

4. COMPORTEMENT DU PARTICIPANT: le sponsor se réserve le droit, à sa seule discrétion, de disqualifier tout(e) participant(e) qui (a) manipule le processus d'inscription ou la participation à la Chasse au trésor ou son déroulement ; (b) transgresse ces lois ou (c) agit d'une manière perturbatrice avec l'intention d'ennuyer, maltraiter, menacer ou harceler tout(e) autre participant(e) ou personne. En vous inscrivant, vous consentez à respecter ce règlement officiel et les décisions du sponsor, qui seront définitives pour toutes les questions se rapportant à la Chasse au trésor. À sa libre appréciation, le sponsor interprète ce règlement officiel et toute autre question relative à la Chasse au trésor ; il se réserve expressément le droit de refuser de remettre la bague à quiconque qui, à l'appréciation du sponsor, aura transgressé ce règlement officiel ou qui par ailleurs ne réunirait pas les conditions satisfaisantes pour gagner.

5. INSTRUCTIONS POUR L'OBTENTION DE LA BAGUE: pour que vous puissiez recevoir votre bague, VOS SOLUTIONS AUX PUZZLES DOIVENT RESTER CONFIDENTIELLES. Vous ne pouvez divulguer aucune solution au risque que le sponsor, modifie, mette fin ou suspende la chasse au trésor, tel que décrit ci-dessous. On vous demandera de donner votre ou vos solution(s) aux puzzles, et de faire une déclaration sous serment de conformité aux conditions de participation et une décharge de responsabilité ou de publicité (là où cela est légal). Si vos réponses s'avèrent exactes, et qu'il est démontré que vous avez utilisé votre intelligence et votre habileté dans le but de résoudre un puzzle de la Chasse au trésor, et à condition que vous répondiez à toutes les autres exigences pour recevoir une bague, on déclarera que vous êtes une personne qui a trouvé. Des exigences de vérification supplémentaires et des instructions pour recevoir la bague peuvent être requises. Les gagnants doivent renvoyer la déclaration sous serment de conformité aux conditions de participation et une décharge de responsabilité ou de publicité dans un délai de vingt-et-un (21) jours à compter de la première tentative de notification de vérification. Si le sponsor le décide, un gagnant potentiel peut être soumis, avec la coopération de ce dernier, à une vérification confidentielle de ses antécédents, destinée à confirmer que les conditions de participation sont remplies et s'assurer que l'utilisation d'une telle personne dans la commercialisation ou la publicité du jeu n'exposera pas le sponsor à un discrédit, mépris, scandale ou ridicule publics ou n'aura pas de répercussion défavorable sur le jeu ou le sponsor, tel que déterminé par le sponsor à sa seule discrétion. S'agissant des gagnants qui sont mineurs, la bague sera remise, au nom du gagnant mineur, à son parent ou tuteur, et des déclarations sous serment et décharges doivent être signées par le parent ou tuteur du gagnant mineur. Les gagnants doivent donner la permission au sponsor de publier le nom et la ville du gagnant à titre de condition pour recevoir la bague, sauf interdiction de la loi. Les gagnants peuvent aussi devoir utiliser leurs noms et soumissions dans des documents publicitaires et de commercialisation dans tous les médias à perpétuité, et peuvent avoir à participer à des événements publicitaires, sauf là où la loi l'interdit. Le sponsor se réserve le droit de ne pas confirmer les gagnants avant la date de clôture.

6. COLLABORATIONS: si vous avez collaboré avec d'autres personnes pendant le concours, chacun des collaborateurs doit répondre à toutes les exigences susmentionnées et fournir tous les documents requis. Les collaborateurs doivent également dégager le sponsor de toute responsabilité relative à l'accord passé entre eux, et si le sponsor encourt des coûts ou frais quelconques, y compris des frais juridiques, découlant de l'accord entre les collaborateurs, tous les collaborateurs consentent à rembourser au sponsor de tels coûts et frais conjointement et solidairement.

7. BAGUES: 100 bagues (sauf pour le Japon) seront disponibles dans la chasse au trésor, dont les valeurs sont les suivantes.

	Valeur estimée	Valeur de substitution en espèces
1 à	1 000 000 US$	300 000 US$
3 à	120 000 US$	40 000 US$
4 à	50 000 US$	15 000 US$
5 à	20 000 US$	6 000 US$
87 à	5 500 US$	1 650 US$

UN FOYER GAGNANT NE PEUT RECEVOIR QU'UNE BAGUE PAR CATÉGORIE DE BAGUE (SOIT UN MAXIMUM DE CINQ BAGUES, UNE POUR CHAQUE CATÉGORIE). Les bagues devant être remises comprennent les bagues représentées ainsi que des bagues qui peuvent ne pas être identiques à celles représentées. Toutes les bagues devant être remises auront des valeurs estimées supérieures ou égales aux valeurs estimées déclarées. Les gagnants peuvent choisir, au lieu de la bague, de recevoir la valeur de substitution en espèces mentionnée ci-dessus. Tous les impôts locaux, provinciaux, d'état ou fédéraux s'appliquant à la réception ou l'utilisation de toute bague et participation à la chasse au trésor relèvent de la seule responsabilité du gagnant. La politique du sponsor, conformément aux règlements du fisc américain, est d'envoyer un formulaire 1099 à tout gagnant résidant aux États-Unis qui a reçu une bague dont la valeur dépasse 600 dollars (US), qui requiert la mention du numéro d'immatriculation à la sécurité sociale du gagnant. Le gagnant est entièrement responsable du paiement de tous les impôts fédéraux et autres taxes conformément aux lois qui s'appliquent dans l'État de sa résidence. Si la loi l'exige, le sponsor se réserve le droit de retenir et de remettre aux autorités fiscales appropriées le montant de tout impôt ou taxe dû. S'agissant des gagnants qui acceptent la bague, et non la valeur de substitution en espèces, la loi peut exiger, conformément au code fiscal américain (tel que déterminé par le sponsor à sa seule discrétion), que le gagnant paie le montant de tout impôt avant de recevoir le prix. S'agissant des gagnants en dehors des États-Unis, la loi fiscale américaine exige le paiement de 30 % de la valeur de la bague reçue, au titre de l'impôt au fisc américain. On vous demandera de fournir au sponsor le paiement de cet impôt avant de recevoir votre bague. D'après la loi japonaise, les gagnants japonais ne recevront pas les prix indiqués ci-dessus, mais ils recevront des prix estimés à la valeur la plus basse entre (a) 100 000 yens ou (b) le prix de vente dans le commerce du livre multiplié par vingt. En outre, les prix offerts à tous les gagnants japonais seront limités à un maximum de deux pour-cent des ventes japonaises brutes du livre.

8. GÉNÉRALITÉS: tous les documents et soumissions au sponsor deviennent la propriété du sponsor et ne seront pas retournés. Le sponsor refuse toute responsabilité relative aux soumissions, correspondances ou tentatives de remise de prix qui sont tardives, perdues ou autrement mal orientées, ou qui ne sont pas soumises conformément à ce règlement officiel. Aucun transfert ou substitution de bague par les gagnants n'est permis, sauf indications dans la présente.

9. RESTRICTIONS SUPPLÉMENTAIRES: en s'inscrivant, les participants (a) consentent à respecter le règlement officiel et les décisions du sponsor qui sont finales et obligatoires à tous les égards ; (b) consentent à dégager le sponsor et ses représentants de toute responsabilité, perte, dommage ou blessure résultant de la participation à cette chasse au trésor, ainsi que de la remise, réception, possession, utilisation et/ou usage impropre de toute bague remise dans la présente et reconnaissent que le sponsor et ses représentants ne sont, ni sont rendus, en aucune manière, responsables (dans la mesure où la loi le permet) de toute garantie, représentation ou garantie expresse ou implicite, en fait ou en droit, relative à toute bague comprenant, mais sans s'y limiter, sa qualité, sa condition mécanique ou adéquation à une fin particulière ; et (c) consentent à utiliser leur nom, photographie et/ ou identification similaire à des fins publicitaires ou promotionnelles sans compensation supplémentaire, sauf si la loi l'interdit. Si une clause de ce règlement officiel est déclarée comme étant non valable, quelle qu'en soit la raison, les autres clauses du règlement officiel demeurent en vigueur. Si le sponsor le décide, un gagnant potentiel peut avoir à se soumettre, avec la coopération de ce dernier, à une vérification confidentielle de ses antécédents permettant de confirmer qu'il remplit toutes les conditions de participation et de s'assurer que l'utilisation d'une telle personne dans la publicité ou commercialisation du jeu n'exposera pas le sponsor à un discrédit, mépris, scandale ou ridicule publics ou n'aura pas de répercussion défavorable sur le jeu ou le sponsor tel que déterminé par le sponsor, à sa seule appréciation.

10. LITIGES: Ce concours est régi par les lois des États-Unis et de l'État de New York, sans tenir compte des doctrines sur les conflits de lois. À titre de condition de participation à ce concours, les participants consentent à ce que tout litige ne pouvant être résolu entre les parties, et les causes d'action naissant de ce concours ou se rapportant à ce dernier, soient résolus individuellement, sans recours à toute forme de recours collectif, exclusivement auprès d'un tribunal situé dans le comté de New York, New York étant compétent. En outre, dans un tel litige, en aucun cas les participants ne seront autorisés à obtenir des compensations pour, et par la présente annulent tout

droit de revendiquer, des dommages-intérêts à titre punitif, indirects ou conséquents, y compris les honoraires d'avocat, autres que les dépenses actuelles payés de la poche du participant (par ex. les frais d'inscription) et le participant renonce en outre à tous les droits d'augmentation ou de multiplication de dommages-intérêts.

11. MODIFICATION OU RÉSILIATION: le sponsor se réserve le droit, à sa seule appréciation, de modifier le concours, le suspendre ou y mettre fin, et/ou de ne pas remettre une bague spécifique, au cas où les solutions de l'événement sont publiées ou autrement communiquées ; ou si un virus, des bogues ou autres causes indépendamment de la volonté du sponsor altèrent la gestion, la sécurité ou le bon déroulement du concours. Le sponsor n'est pas responsable des inscriptions tardives, incomplètes ou mal orientées ; du mauvais fonctionnement du système informatique, des lignes téléphoniques et de l'équipement ou des programmes, ou d'autres erreurs ; des pannes ou retards dans les transmissions informatiques ou connexions réseau ; des difficultés pour télécharger quoi que ce soit du site Web ; des dommages causés à l'ordinateur du participant ou de toute autre personne, en relation avec, ou résultant de la participation au concours ou le/du téléchargement de tout document ou tout autre problème technique se rapportant à ces inscriptions.

12. PUBLICATION DES GAGNANTS: après la date de clôture de la chasse au trésor, les noms des gagnants seront publiés sur le site Web.

13. SPONSOR: le sponsor de cette chasse au trésor est Treasure Trove, Inc., 161 Cherry Street, New Canaan, CT 06840.

DER SCHATZFUND: Geheimnisse des Alchemisten Dar, Fähigkeitenwettbewerb - Offizielle Regeln

1. TEILNAHME AN DIESER AKTION (die „Schatzsuche"): Besorgen Sie sich ein Exemplar des Buches „A Treasurer's Trove": Secrets of the Alchemist Dar (Der Schatzfund: Geheimnisse des Alchemisten Dar) von Michael Stadther (nachstehend das „Buch"). Gehen Sie auf die Website www.alchemistdar.com, um sich für das Spiel zu registrieren. In dem Buch enthalten sind Rätsel und Hinweise, die Sie lösen müssen. Wenn Sie glauben, eines der Rätsel gelöst zu haben, wissen Sie, wie Sie Ihren Ring einlösen können (Anweisungen zur Einlösung gehören zum Puzzel). Die Rätsel und Hinweise können Sie mit Ihrem Verstand und Ihren Fähigkeiten lösen (Glück spielt in diesem Teil der Schatzsuche keine Rolle.) Wenn Sie ein Rätsel lösen und Sie die Berechtigungskriterien erfüllen, folgen Sie den Anweisungen für die Einlösung. Sie bekommen dann nach einer Prüfung den angegebenen Ring. Sie müssen den Anspruch persönlich geltend machen. Einreichungen über Vertreter oder Dritte sind nicht zulässig. Das Buch wurde der Öffentlichkeit zum ersten Mal am 26./27. September 2006 zugänglich gemacht. Die Schatzsuche läuft so lange weiter, bis alle Rätsel gelöst und die Gewinner bestimmt sind oder bis zum 30./31. Dezember 2009 (der „Endtermin"), je nachdem, was früher eintritt.

2. TEILNAHMEBERECHTIGUNG: Allen rechtmäßigen Einwohnern der 50 Bundesstaaten der Vereinigten Staaten, einschließlich des District of Columbia (außer Bewohnern der Staaten Maryland, North Dakota und Vermont), des Vereinigten Königreichs, Kanadas (in Quebec ungültig), Irlands, Australiens, Neuseelands, Frankreichs, Deutschlands, Singapurs, Hongkongs und Japans. Nach japanischem Recht gilt für die Gewinner in Japan gemäß unten stehender Erläuterungen eine andere Preisstruktur. Beachten Sie bitte, dass sich jeder das Buch beschaffen und teilnehmen kann, indem er versucht, die Rätsel zu lösen, auf Grund rechtlicher Beschränkungen und der mit der Beschaffung der rechtlichen Freigabe verbundenen Kosten können aber nur Bewohner dieser gerichtlichen Zuständigkeitsbereiche Ringe bekommen. Gewinner könnten eine eidesstattliche Erklärung abgeben und schwören müssen, diese Teilnahmevoraussetzungen zu erfüllen. Mitarbeiter des Sponsors, ihre unmittelbaren Familienmitglieder und im Haushalt lebende Personen (ob verwandt oder nicht) und Vertreter, die an der Entwicklung dieser Schatzsuche mitgewirkt haben, dürfen nicht teilnehmen.

3. DETAILS: Die Lösungen für alle Rätsel in dem Buch wurden erfasst und werden an einem sicheren Ort aufbewahrt. Die Lösungen werden nach dem Endtermin entweder auf der Website oder in einer nachfolgenden Veröffentlichung bekannt gegeben werden. Sie können auf der folgenden Website mehr über das Buch und die Schatzsuche erfahren: www.thealchemistdar.com.

4. VERHALTEN DER TEILNEHMER: Der Sponsor behält sich das Recht vor, in seinem eigenen Ermessen jeden Teilnehmer disqualifizieren zu können, der (a) den Zugangsprozess oder die Teilnahme an oder den Ablauf der Schatzsuche manipuliert, (b) diese Regeln verletzt oder (c) zerstörerisch mit dem Ziel der Verärgerung, Ausnutzung, Bedrohung oder Belästigung eines anderen Teilnehmers oder einer anderen Person handelt. Durch die Teilnahme erklären Sie sich einverstanden, diese Offiziellen Regeln einzuhalten und sich an die Entscheidungen des Sponsors zu halten, die in jeder Hinsicht zu allen Aspekten der Schatzsuche endgültig sind. Es liegt allein im Ermessen des Sponsors, diese Offiziellen Regeln und alle anderen Aspekte der Schatzsuche zu interpretieren, und dieser behält sich ausdrücklich das Recht vor, es abzulehnen, einem Teilnehmer den Ring zu verleihen, der nach Meinung des Sponsors diese Offiziellen Regeln verletzt oder anderweitig seine Gewinnberechtigung nicht zufrieden stellend darlegt.

5. ANWEISUNGEN FÜR DAS EINLÖSEN: Um Ihren Ring zu bekommen, MÜSSEN SIE IHRE LÖSUNGEN DER RÄTSEL VERTRAULICH BEHANDELN. Sie dürfen keine Lösungen bekannt machen, andernfalls kann der Sponsor die Schatzsuche wie unten beschrieben abändern, beenden oder aussetzen. Sie werden gebeten werden, Ihre Lösung(en) der Rätsel anzugeben und eine eidesstattliche Erklärung der Teilnahmeberechtigung und Haftung/Freigabe zur Bekanntmachung (wo dies legal ist) zu unterzeichen. Falls Ihre Antworten bei der Prüfung derselben als richtig bestimmt werden und entschieden wird, dass Sie Ihren Verstand und Ihre Fähigkeiten eingesetzt haben, um ein Rätsel der Schatzsuche zu lösen, vorausgesetzt Sie sind in jeglicher anderen Hinsicht berechtigt, den Ring zu bekommen, werden Sie zu einem Finder des Schatzes erklärt. Zusätzliche Anforderungen an die Prüfung und Anweisungen für das Einlösen können notwendig sein. Die Gewinner müssen die eidesstattliche Erklärung der Teilnahmeberechtigung und Haftung/Freigabe an die Öffentlichkeit innerhalb von einundzwanzig (21) Tagen nach der ersten versuchten Benachrichtigung über die Überprüfung zurückschicken. Falls der Sponsor dies wünscht, kann ein möglicher Preisgewinner sich einer vertraulichen Hintergrundprüfung unterziehen lassen und darin zusammenarbeiten müssen, um die Teilnahmeberechtigung zu bestätigen und um sicherzustellen, dass der Einsatz dieser Person in der Bewerbung oder Reklame für das Spiel den Sponsor nicht öffentlich in Misskredit bringt, in Missachtung, Skandale oder Spott verwickelt oder ein schlechtes Bild des Sponsors zeichnet – dies kann der Sponsor in seinem eigenen Ermessen bestimmen. Für Gewinner, die noch nicht volljährig sind, wird der Ring im Namen des Finders an seine/ihre Eltern oder Vormund vergeben, und die eidesstattlichen Erklärungen und Freigaben müssen in dem Fall von den Elternteil des Finders oder dem Vormund unterzeichnet sein. Die Gewinner müssen dem Sponsor die Genehmigung erteilen, als Bedingung für die Aushändigung des Rings den Namen und die Heimatort des Finders veröffentlichen zu dürfen, außer dies ist rechtlich nicht zulässig. Die Gewinner müssen eventuell auch ihre Namen und Einreichungen an Werbe- und Marketingmaterialien in allen Medien auf unbegrenzte Dauer nutzen lassen und müssen möglicherweise an Werbeveranstaltungen teilnehmen, außer dies ist rechtlich nicht zulässig. Der Sponsor behält sich das Recht vor, die Bestätigung der Gewinner erst nach dem Endtermin vorzunehmen.

6. KOOPERATIONEN: Falls Sie bei Ihren Bemühungen mit anderen Personen zusammengearbeitet haben, muss jeder der Teilnehmer alle vorstehend erwähnten Anforderungen erfüllen und alle erforderlichen Dokumente abgeben. Die kooperierenden Spieler müssen den Sponsor auch von jeder Haftung in Zusammenhang mit ihrer Vereinbarung untereinander entbinden. Wenn dem Sponsor Kosten oder Aufwendungen in Zusammenhang mit der Vereinbarung der kooperierenden Spieler entstehen, einschließlich rechtlicher Aufwendungen, stimmen alle kooperierenden Spieler zu, dem Sponsor alle diese Kosten und Aufwendungen einzel- und gesamtschuldnerisch zu erstatten.

7. RINGE: 100 Ringe (außer für Japan) werden für die Schatzsuche mit den folgenden Werten vorhanden sein:

	Geschätzter Wert	Wert bei Barauszahlung
1 zu	US$1.000.000	US$300.000
3 zu	US$ 120.000	US$ 40.000
4 zu	US$ 50.000	US$ 15.000
5 zu	US$ 20.000	US$ 6.000
87 zu	US$ 5.500	US$ 1.650

ES KANN NUR EIN RING PRO RINGEBENE UND HAUSHALT VERGEBEN WERDEN (INSGESAMT FÜNF RINGE MAXIMAL, EINER FÜR JEDE EBENE). Zu verleihende Ringe sind u.a. die abgebildeten Ringe, aber auch Ringe, die nicht den Abbildungen entsprechen. Alle zu verleihenden Ringe haben einen geschätzten Wert, der den angegebenen geschätzten Werten entspricht oder über diese hinausgeht. Gewinner können an Stelle des Rings die Barauszahlung mit den oben angegebenen Preisen wählen. Alle Bundes-, bundesstaatlichen, Bezirks- und Lokalsteuern, die mit dem Erhalt oder der Nutzung eines Rings und der Teilnahme an der Schatzsuche einhergehen, liegen in der alleinigen Verantwortung des Finders. Die Politik des Sponsors ist es, in Übereinstimmung mit den Bestimmungen der US-Finanzbehörde, ein Formular 1099 an jeden in den USA ansässigen Gewinner zu schicken, der einen Ring im Wert von mehr als $600 (USD) erhält, da hierbei die Angabe der Sozialversicherungsnummer erforderlich ist. Es liegt allein in der Verantwortung des Gewinners, alle Bundessteuern und alle anderen Steuern im Einklang mit den im Bundesstaat des Wohnsitzes geltenden Gesetzen zu zahlen. Falls gesetzlich erforderlich behält sich der Sponsor das Recht der Einbehaltung und Weiterleitung des Betrages der fälligen Steuer oder Steuern an die entsprechende Steuerbehörde vor. Im Hinblick auf die Gewinner, die den Ring und nicht das Bargeld nehmen, kann es gemäß dem Einkommensteuerrecht der USA (gemäß Feststellung durch den Sponsor in seinem alleinigen Ermessen) rechtlich notwendig sein, dass der Gewinner des Preises den entsprechenden Steuerbetrag vor Annahme des Preises zahlt. Für Gewinner außerhalb der Vereinigten Staaten – das US-amerikanische Recht verlangt die Zahlung von 30% des Wertes des erhaltenen Rings als Steuern an die US-Finanzbehörde. Sie werden gebeten werden, dem Sponsor vor Annahme Ihres Ringes diese Steuerzahlung zukommen zu lassen. Gemäß japanischem Recht erhalten japanische Gewinner nicht die oben beschriebenen Preise, sondern erhalten die Preise zu einem Wert, der geringer ist als (a) 100.000 Yen oder (b) der Verkaufspreis des Buches multipliziert mit zwanzig. Des Weiteren werden alle japanischen Gewinnern angebotene Preise sein maximal zwei Prozent des Bruttoumsatzes des Buches in Japan gekappt.

8. ALLGEMEINES: Alle Materialien und Einreichungen an den Sponsor werden Eigentum des Sponsors und werden nicht zurückgegeben. Der Sponsor übernimmt keine Haftung für Einreichungen, Korrespondenz oder versuchte Einlösungen, die zu spät eintreffen, verloren gehen oder anderweitig fehlgeleitet werden oder die nicht im Einklang mit diesen Offiziellen Regeln eingereicht werden. Keine Übertragung oder Erstattung von Ringen ist durch die Gewinner zulässig, außer wie hierin beschrieben.

9. ZUSÄTZLICHE BESCHRÄNKUNGEN: Durch die Teilnahme (a) stimmen die Teilnehmer zu, sich an die offiziellen Regeln und die Entscheidungen des Sponsors zu halten, die in jeder Hinsicht endgültig und verbindlich sind, (b) stimmen die Teilnehmer zu, den Sponsor und die Vertreter von aller Haftung, Verlust, Schaden oder Verletzung schadlos zu halten, die sich aus der Teilnahme an dieser Schatzsuche ergibt, aber auch aus der Zuerkennung, dem Erhalt, dem Besitz, der Nutzung und/oder dem Missbrauch eines Rings, der hiernach zugesprochen wurde und erkennen an, dass der Sponsor und die Vertreter keine Garantien, Darstellung, Gewährleistungen, weder ausdrücklich noch implizit, weder tatsächlich noch gesetzlich, bezüglich eines jeglichen Rings gemacht haben oder auf jegliche Art und Weise dafür verantwortlich oder haftbar sind (in dem per Gesetz zulässigen Maße), einschließlich, aber nicht beschränkt auf seine Qualität, seinen mechanischen Zustand oder seine Eignung für einen bestimmten Zweck und (c) stimmt der Teilnehmer der Nutzung seines/ihres Namens, Fotos und/oder Bildes zu Werbe- oder Promotionzwecken ohne zusätzliche Vergütung zu, außer dies ist per Gesetz nicht zulässig. Falls eine Bestimmung dieser offiziellen Regeln aus irgendeinem Grund für ungültig erklärt wird, bleiben die übrigen offiziellen Regeln vollständig in Kraft und rechtsgültig. Falls der Sponsor dies wünscht, kann ein möglicher Preisgewinner sich einer vertraulichen Hintergrundprüfung unterziehen lassen und darin zusammenarbeiten müssen, um die Teilnahmeberechtigung zu bestätigen und um sicherzustellen, dass der Einsatz dieser Person in der Bewerbung oder Reklame für das Spiel den Sponsor nicht öffentlich in Misskredit bringt, in Missachtung, Skandale oder Spott verwickelt oder ein schlechtes Bild des Spiels oder des Sponsors zeichnet – dies kann der Sponsor in seinem eigenen Ermessen bestimmen.

10. STREITIGKEITEN: Dieser Wettbewerb unterliegt den Gesetzen der Vereinigten Staaten und des Bundesstaates New York, ohne Rücksicht auf Grundsätze zu Rechtskonflikten. Als Bedingung für die Teilnahme an diesem Wettbewerb stimmen die Teilnehmer zu, dass alle Streitigkeiten, die nicht zwischen den Parteien gelöst werden können und Klagegründe, die sich aus oder in Zusammenhang mit diesem Wettbewerb ergeben, einzeln, ohne Rückgriff auf eine Art der Sammelklage, ausschließlich vor einem Gericht beizulegen sind, das sich im Bezirk New York, Bundesstaat New York befindet und zuständig ist. Des Weiteren ist es in einem solchen Rechtsstreit Teilnehmern unter keinen Umständen erlaubt, Schadenersatzteile zu erwirken für und er verzichtet hiermit auf alle Rechte, Strafzuschläge zum Schadenersatz, Ersatz für beiläufig entstandene Schäden oder für Folgeschäden zu fordern, einschließlich Anwaltskosten, mit Ausnahme der tatsächlichen Auslagen des Teilnehmers (z.B. Kosten in Zusammenhang mit der Teilnahme), und der Teilnehmer verzichtet des Weiteren auf alle Rechte, Schadenersatz zu vervielfachen oder zu erhöhen.

11. ÄNDERUNG ODER KÜNDIGUNG: Der Sponsor behält sich das Recht vor, in seinem eigenen Ermessen den Wettbewerb zu ändern, auszusetzen oder zu kündigen und/oder einen speziellen Ring nicht zu verleihen, falls Lösungen veröffentlicht werden oder anderweitig weitergegeben werden, oder falls ein Virus, Programmfehler oder ähnliche Ursachen, der nicht in der Kontrolle des Sponsors liegen, die Verwaltung, Sicherheit oder ordnungsgemäße Durchführung des Wettbewerbs unmöglich machen. Der Sponsor ist nicht für zu spät eingegangene, verloren gegangene, unvollständige oder falsch adressierte Teilnahmen, Computersystem-, Telefonleitungs-, Ausrüstungs- oder Programmfehlfunktionen oder andere Fehler, Ausfälle oder Verzögerungen in der Computerübertragung oder Netzwerkverbindungen, Problemen beim Download von Inhalten von der Website, Schäden am Computer des Teilnehmers oder einer anderen Person im Zusammenhang mit oder als Ergebnis aus der Teilnahme oder des Herunterladens von Materialien oder für irgendwelche anderen technischen Probleme verantwortlich, die mit der Teilnahme in Zusammenhang stehen.

12. VERÖFFENTLICHUNG DER GEWINNER: Nach dem Endtermin der Schatzsuche werden die Gewinner auf der Website veröffentlicht.

13. SPONSOR: Der Sponsor dieser Schatzsuche ist Treasure Trove, Inc., 161 Cherry Street, New Canaan, CT, 06840.

「埋蔵物: アルケミスト・ダー(Alchemist Dar)の秘訣」宝探しコンテスト公式ルール

1. 本販売促進 (以後「宝探し」)参加の仕方: まずマイケル・スタッドサー(Michael Stadther)の本、「埋蔵物: アルケミスト・ダー(Alchemist Dar)の秘訣 (以後「本」)をお買い上げください。次にウェブサイトwww.alchemistdar.comへ行き、登録を行ってください。本には、パズルとそれを解くためのヒントが含まれています。どれか一つパズルが解けたら、リングの取得方法が分かるはずです(リング取得方法もパズルになっています)。パズルとヒントは知力と応用で解けます(本宝探しには答が偶然当たったということはありません)。パズルが解け、応募資格要求事項を満足させた後、リング取得方法の指示に従ってください。照合がされ、指定されたリングがもらえます。これは参加者自身が行ってください。代理人や第三者を通した請求は無効です。本は一般向けに2006年9月26/27日(米国東部標準時)以降購入できます。宝探しはすべてのパズルが解かれ、入賞者の資格照合立証が行なわれるまで、または2009年12月30/31日(「終了日」)までのどちらか早い方の日付まで継続されます。

2. 応募資格: ワシントンD.C.を含む米国50州(メリーランド、ノースダコタ、バーモントの住民は例外)、英国、カナダ(ケベックは無効)、アイルランド、オーストラリア、ニュージーランド、フランス、ドイツ、シンガポール、香港、および日本の合法的住民が本コンテストに応募できます。日本の法律では、日本の入賞者は以下に示す別の賞品システムに従います。本を購入しコンテストに参加してパズルを解くのは誰が行っても構いませんが、法的な制限と法的認可に伴う経費の関係上、リングがもらえるのは上述の管轄権内の住民に限られます。入賞者は、応募資格要求事項を遵守する旨の宣誓供述書を提出するよう要求される場合があります。スポンサーの従業員、その肉親や家族構成員(親戚であるか否かに関係なく)、および本宝探しの作成に参加した代理人には応募資格はありません。

3. 詳細: 本の中のパズルの回答はすべて安全な場所に記録・保管されています。回答は、終了日以降、ウェブサイトまたは出版物のいずれかで発表されます。本と宝探しの詳細については、ウェブサイトwww.thealchemistdar.comをご覧ください。

4. 参加者の行為: スポンサーは自身の裁量により、(a) 宝探しへの応募プロセス、参加、または運営に不正に干渉する参加者、(b) 本ルールに違反する参加者、または (c) 他参加者を不愉快にさせる、困らせる、脅す、または苦しめる目的で破壊的な行為を行う参加者の資格を剥奪する権利を保有します。あなたは、本コンテストに参加することにより、本文書の公式ルールおよびスポンサーの決定に伴うすべての拘束に合意したことになり、宝探しに関するすべての面でそれが最終判断となります。スポンサーは本文書の公式ルールや宝探しに関する他の諸点の解釈の面で 完全に自由裁量権を有し、スポンサーの裁量で本文書の公式ルールに違反していると考えられる参加者、または入賞資格を充分満足していないと考えられる参加者へのリングの贈呈を拒否できる権利を有します。

5. 取得方法: リングを受け取るには、パズルの回答を他の人に絶対におしえないでください。回答を他の人と共有しないでください。そのような行為を行うと、スポンサーは以下説明のように、宝探しを修正、中止、または停止する場合があります。パズルが解けた場合、その回答を提出し、応募資格に関する宣誓供述書および合法的な公表責任免除許可書を提出するよう要求されます。正しい答えであると照合立証され、自身の知力と応用を使って宝探しのパズルを解いたと判断され、他のあらゆる面でリングを受け取る資格があると認められた場合に、あなたが答の発見者であると宣言されます。追加的な資格照合立証事項と取得方法がさらに要求される場合もあります。入賞者は、最初の照合立証通知から21日以内に応募資格に関する宣誓供述書および公表責任免除許可書を提出しなければなりません。スポンサーの判断により、入賞候補者は極秘の身元調査のために資料を提出、協力などをするように要求される場合もあります。それは、応募資格を確証し、そのような参加者をゲームの広告や宣伝に起用しても、スポンサーの名誉が公的に傷つけられたり、スポンサーが軽蔑、スキャンダル、または嘲笑の対象にならないこと、またはゲームおよびスポンサーに悪い影響が及ばないことを、スポンサーの裁量による判断で確認するためです。未成年入賞者は、発見者本人の名前でその親または合法的保護者にリングが渡され、発見者本人の親または合法的な保護者が宣誓供述書および免除許可書に署名してください。法律で禁止されない限り、リングを受け取る条件として、入賞者は本人の氏名と居住地の公表許可をスポンサーに提供しなければなりません。法律で禁じられている場合は例外として、入賞者は氏名や提出物を広告やマーケティング用の資料としてあらゆるマスコミで永久的に使用する許可を要求される場合もあり、公表の際の催し物に参加するよう要求される場合もあります。スポンサーは、最終日の後まで入賞者の応募資格照合立証を確認しないでおく権利も有します。

6. 共同参加: 他の人と共同でパズルを解いた場合は、共同参加者全員が前述の要求事項を遵守し、すべての必要書類を提出しなければなりません。共同参加者は互いの間で交わされた合意に関連してあらゆる責任からスポンサーを免除しなければならず、共同参加者間の合意に関連してスポンサ

ーに経費や出費(法律面の出費も含む)が生じた場合は、共同参加者全員が連帯でそのような経費や出費の全額をスポンサーに返済することに合意しなければなりません。

7. リング: 宝探しで入手可能なリングは100個(日本は例外)で、その価値は以下の通りです。

	評定価格	現金払額
1 @	1,000,000ドル	300,000ドル
3 @	120,000ドル	40,000ドル
4 @	50,000ドル	15,000ドル
5 @	20,000ドル	6,000ドル
87 @	5,500ドル	1,650ドル

入賞者は家族単位で各レベルにつき1個のリングしか受け取れません(各レベルで1個ですから、最高で5個です)。贈呈されるリングには、写真などで提示されたリングおよび写真などで提示されたリングとは全く同一ではないリングが含まれます。贈呈されるリングはすべて、評定価格またはそれ以上の価値を有します。入賞者はリングの代わりに上記の現金額を受け取ることもできます。リングの受領または使用および宝探しへの参加に伴って生じる連邦税、州税、地方税の支払いはすべて入賞者の責任です。米国内国歳入庁の規則を遵守するため、600米国ドルを超える価値のリングを受け取った米国在住入賞者には、スポンサーは書式1099を送付します。居住州の法律に従って連邦税や他の税金を納めるのは入賞者の責任です。法的に要求される場合、スポンサーは支払われるべき税額を天引きし、適切な税当局に送金する権利を有します。現金ではなくリングを受け取る入賞者に関しては、スポンサーの裁量に従い、米国内国歳入法の下に、賞品を受け取る前に納税する必要が生じる場合もあります。米国外入賞者は、米国税法に従い、受け取るリングの価値の30%を税金として米国内国歳入庁へ納めなければなりません。入賞者は、リングを受け取る前に、相当金額をスポンサーに提出するよう要求されます。日本の入賞者は日本の法律に従い、上記の賞品は受け取りません。代わりに、(a) 10万円 (b) または 本の小売価格の20倍のうちいずれか少ない方の価格の賞品を受け取ります。さらに、日本の入賞者に贈与される賞品の相当全額は、最高で日本における本の総売上の2%までとなります。

8. 一般事項: スポンサーに退出される資料や提出物はすべてスポンサーの財産となり、返却されません。提出物、往復文書、あるいは遅延、喪失、または宛名を書き誤った賞品取得の申し込み、または本文書の公式ルールに従って要求されなかった取得申し込みに関しては、スポンサーは一切責任を負いません。本文書に記述されている場合以外は、リングを他の人に譲渡したり現金に替えることは入賞者には認められていません。

9. 追加制限事項: 参加者は、本コンテストに参加することにより、(a) 本文書の公式ルールとすべての面で最終的で拘束力を持つスポンサーの決定に拘束されることに合意し、(b) 宝探しへの参加およびリングの贈呈、受領、所有、使用、および/または誤認に伴って生じる責任、損失、損傷、または権利の侵害からスポンサーとその代理人を免除することに合意し、品質、物理的状態、または特別目的への適合性を含むがこれに限定されないような、リングに関するいかなる担保責任、表明、または保証も、明示的であれ黙示的であれ、事実であれ法律的であれ、スポンサーもその代理人も法律の許す範囲でいかなる形でも責任を負わないこと(法が許可する範囲内で)を承認し、(c) 法律で禁止されない範囲内で、氏名、写真および/または肖像を追加報酬なしに広告や販売促進目的に使用することにも同意します。本文書の公式ルールの一規定が何らかの理由で無効であると宣言されたとしても、残りの規定の効力は元のまま完全に維持されます。スポンサーの選択により、入賞候補者は極秘の身元調査のために資料を提出、協力するように要求される場合があります。それは、応募資格を確証し、そのような参加者をゲームの広告や宣伝に起用しても、スポンサーの名誉が公的に傷ついたり、スポンサーが軽蔑、スキャンダル、または嘲笑の対象にならないこと、またはゲームやスポンサーに悪い影響が及ばないことをスポンサーの判断で確認するためです。

10. 論争事項. 本コンテストは、抵触法原則とは無関係に、米国およびニューヨーク州の法律に準じるものです。参加者は、コンテスト参加の条件として、当事者間で解決できないすべての論争および本コンテストが原因でまたはそれと関連して生じる訴訟原因は、いかなる形の集団訴訟にも訴えることなく、ひたすら管轄権を有すニューヨーク州ニューヨーク郡(New York County, New York)の裁判所で、個人的に解決されるべきことに合意します。さらに、そのような論争において、参加者は実際に生じた小口費用(例えばコンテストへの参加に伴う経費)以外、いかなる事情の下にあっても、弁護士料も含めて懲罰的損害賠償、付随的損害賠償、間接損害などに関する報償を許可されてはなりません。従って参加者はそのような請求権をここに一切放棄し、さらに損害賠償額の倍数化または増加を行なう権利もすべて放棄します。

11. 修正または期間満了: スポンサーは、回答が公表または共有された場合、またはウイルス、バグ、その他スポンサーの管理範囲を超えた他の原因によりコンテストの管理、安全、公正が破壊された場合は、スポンサーの裁量により、コンテストを修正、停止、中止する権利、および/または特定のリングを贈呈しない権利を有します。スポンサーは、遅延、喪失、不完全、または宛名を書き誤ったコンテスト参加申し込み、コンピューター・システム、電話線、装置、またはプログラムの不良やエラー、コンピューターによる送信やネットワーク接続の失敗または遅延、ウェブサイトからのダウンロードの問題、参加または資料のダウンロードに関連してまたはそれが原因で生じたコンテスト参加者のコンピューターまたは他の人のコンピューターの損傷、またはコンテスト参加に関連して生じる他の技術的な問題には全く責任を持ちません。

12. 入賞者の公表: 入賞者は、宝探しの終了日以降ウェブサイトで発表されます。

13. スポンサー: 本宝探しのスポンサーはトレジャー・トローブ社(Treasure Trove, Inc.)、郵便番号06840 コネチカット州ニューケイナン市チェリー・ストリート161番地(161 Cherry Street, New Canaan, CT 06840)です。

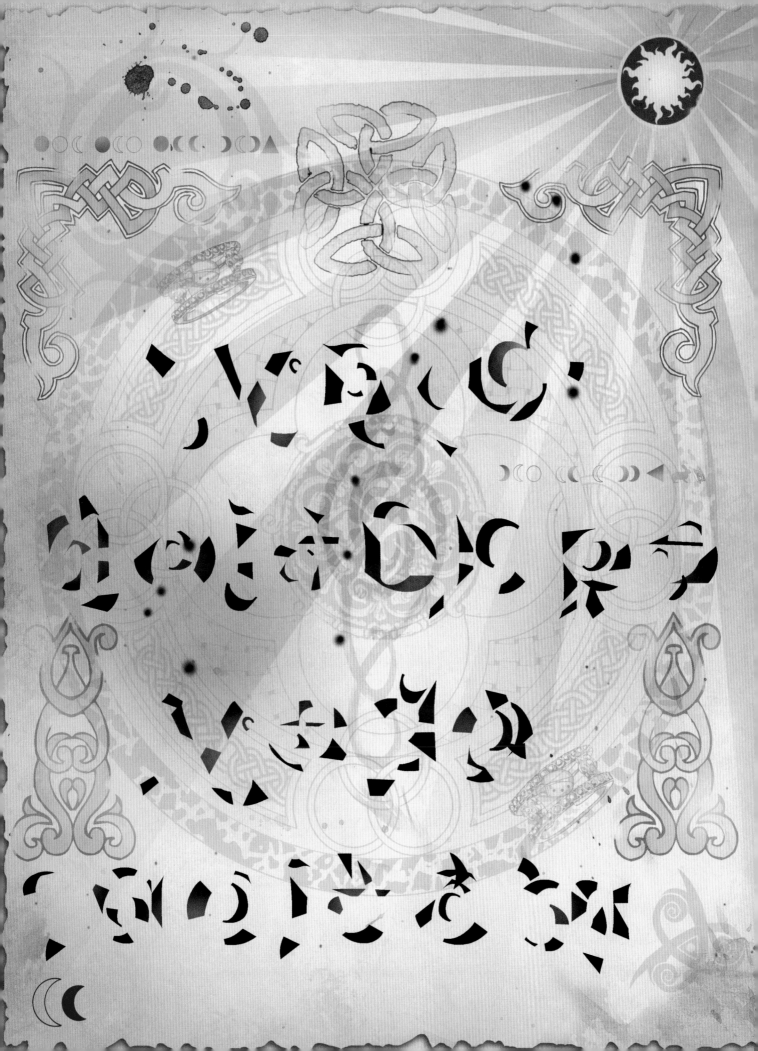

☼ Light Spell

Reversi Luna

Lunar orb on your

Around your circular

A celestial dance you must

And reverse your current

This Spell No Work

Light Spell of Reversi Luna

Purpose

To reverse a moon's orbit. Laxo orbis.
Caster must be pure of hart.

Effect on Caster

Trepidation, longings of the hart.

Distance of spell effect

Unto the moon.

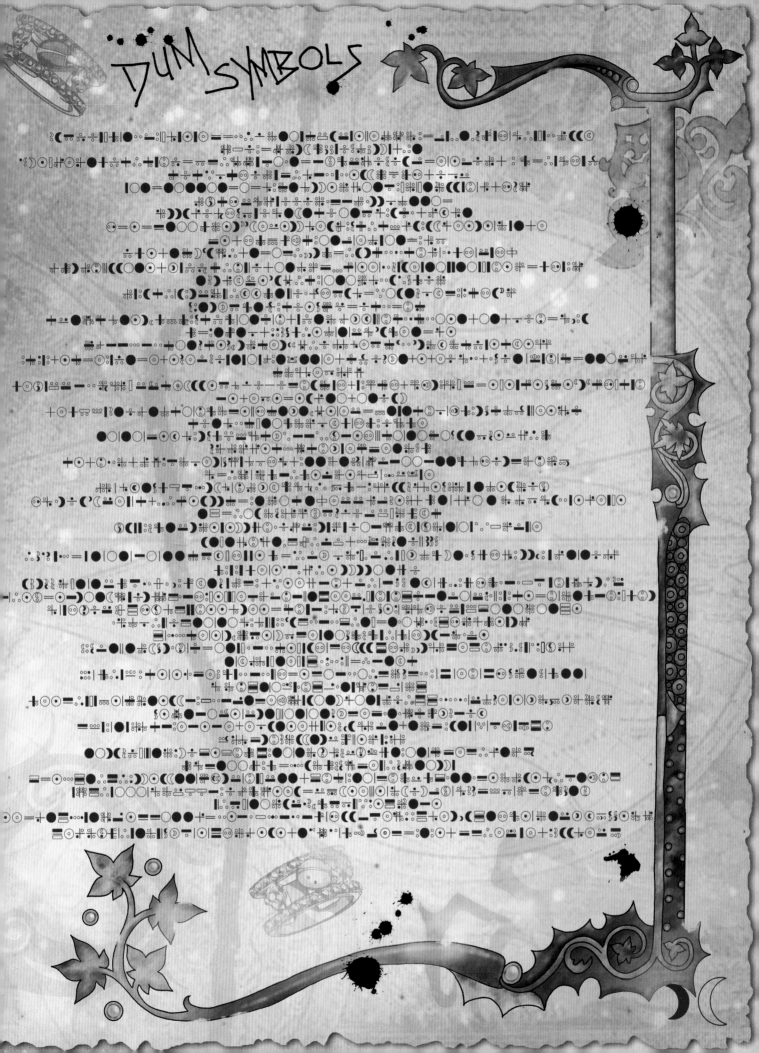

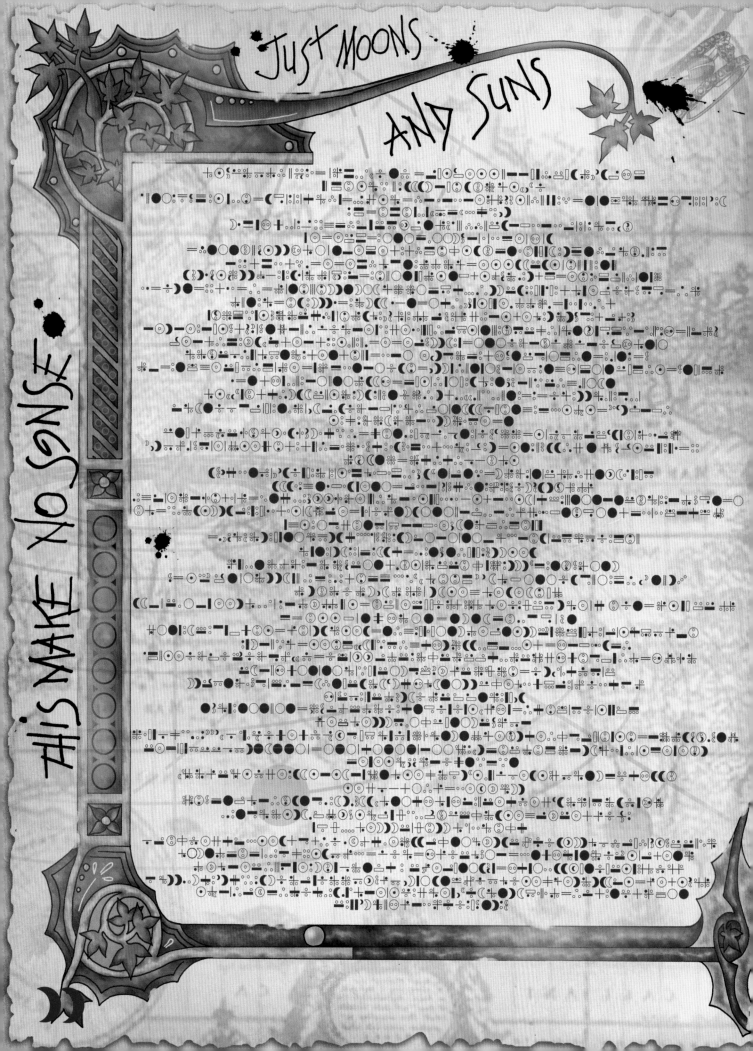

Purpose

To create a Fairy Ring of Eternal Life. Orbis Vita.

Effect on Caster

Forgettyng one's owne selfe for another.
Generaso Impelloso.

Distance of spell effect

From nothyngness to sumthyngness.

Chant Spell

Summon a Ring

Purpose

To carry a Fairy Ring of Eternal Life to Caster. Apello Lecto.

Effect on Caster

Eternal bliss. Joie Aeternum.

Distance of spell effect

From sumthyngness unto givyngness unto the given.

ECLIPSE

ECLIPSE

Fairies breath now began

It will you all replace

GOOD FAIRIES

FAIRIES S GOOD

Death

Life yields to your embrace

And now it's done

ECLIPSE

ECLIPSE

Eclipse Spell

GOOD FAIRIES GOOD FAIRIES GOOD FAIRIES GOOD FAIRIES

Purpose

Action of spell on Fates of Go... ...ro Spiritus:

Spell kill good fairies pet fairy ring

Effect on Caster

Sleep with m...y dreams. Vita Excessum.

Uh? Nothing bad

Distance of spell effect

To the edges of the Eærth.

Open
FAIRIES
LAND

Fairies in the cave   I command you all

Fairies in the cave → ↑ And heed my call

↓ Take flight now leave

Eclipse Spell

OPEN
FAIRIES
EARTH

LET US OUT TO GET RINGS!

Purpose

Bidden Fairies homeward; to their proper place.
Returnam domus.

Effect on Caster

Beware: Cwic ær buffetts an evil caster.

Distance of spell effect

Evrywhere above ground.

ECLIPSE

ECLIPSE

MAY HUMANS LEAVE

Growth anew

I command you

GROW

MOLD

Become now past

This spell I cast

NO FOOD FOR THEM

ECLIPSE

ECLIPSE

Eclipse Spell

MOLD

Purpose

Action of spell upon food.

Effect on Caster

Same as the purpose of the spell.

Distance of spell effect

To the edges of the Earth.

Chant Spell
Arise

Purpose

Restoren flyht to winged creatures.
Volo denuo.

Effect on Caster

A feeling of lyghtness. Gravno brevis.

Distance of spell effect

Wheresoever theyr be flyhing.

- **Fly and arise**
- **Spell l utter**
- **Into the skies**
- **Wings aflutter**

sky   structure

h

xy

Descend

Purpose

Grounden flyht of winged creatures. Plummeterra.

Effect on Caster

A terrible hevvyness

Distance of spell effect

Unto the darkest Deeps close by the caster.
Can be used but once a moon.

- Rise and soar

- Your wings ascend

- Fly no more

- You now descend

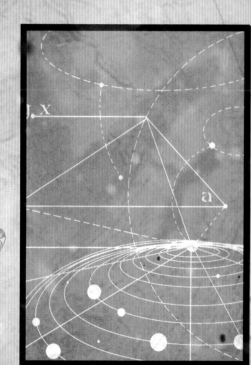

Chant Spell
Crevasse

Purpose

Ætrappen profundum.

Creaytn a deep impassable chasm in the Eærth, preventen ye enemies from approachen.

Effect on Caster

A pulling down & near to the chasm.

Distance of spell effect

Twixt the horizon long and broad.

🜚 Ground will shake

🜚 And none can pass

🜚 This spell to make

🜚 A deep crevasse

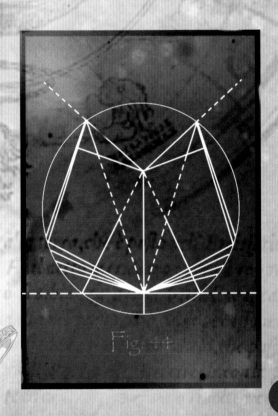

Fig. 44

Time of the Syzygies

Prophesy tells that in the Year of Ye Hest 3243, three syzygies will occur within a night, a day, and the next night. Only then can the powerful Eclipse Spells be cast.

Syzygy

Pronunciation: **si-ze-jee**

Plural: **syzygies**

Etymology: Old Hest syzygia, conjunction from yoked together, from syn-zygon.

Ye near-straight line twixt three celæstial bodies, as sumtyme be ye sun, moon, and ye Eæerth tugethr.

Solar Eclipse

Pronunciation: **so-ler ee-klips**

Etymology: Old Hest Solar (Sun), and eclipses from ekleipein, to omit, fail, suffer, eclipse, from ex and leipein, to leave.

Moon blocken sun from Eæerth.
Ye allway or partway obscuring by ye Moon of sunlight showne on ye Eæerth.

Lunar Eclipse

Pronunciation: **lu-ner ee-klips**

Etymology: Middle Hest, Lunaris, from luna, moon, and eclipses, as showne above.

Eæerth blocken sun from moon.
Ye allway or partway obscuring by Eæerth of sunlight showne on ye moon.

Eclipse Spells

These spells be save for The Tyme of The Umbra and The Occultation. These be spells with hydden powers that can be used for Good or Evil and become especially vile during The Tyme of eclipses threes.

Caster recites all wyrds during eclipse and last wyrd at the moment full.

▪◆◆◆◆●(▲◆◆◆▼▲◆◆—●◆◆◆◆◆▮◆▮▲◆◆◆◆◆◆

WS MAKE WORK DOOD

Light Spells

Ye most special verses in these pages be those for creating a Light Spell. These lines be writ in a lingua onliest knowable to The First Sages of the lectio antiquuis. As seeds fly on gossamer wings in springtyme, Light Spells on paper come and go with the wind. So old Hest sages do prescribe: memorize evry thyng. Be Ye Bok, Be Ye Never Lost. Libris Memoria.

)◆(▲◆◆▮◆◆—◆◆◆◆▮(▲◆▲▼)◆◆▮◆◆)▮◆◆)▼◆◆▲◆◆◆◆◆◆ ●○

Chant Spells

These be spells of the simplest fare, writ by The Sages for students at one Tyme. All can be accomplished with greate success by any human, Fairy, elf, or other Creature. With minde in reddyness, the caster recites all wyrds in full voice.

...oncentration rewards. In Allways, such Spells reap greate benefit for all who wish the Greate Forest well. It is said that with vere much Study and Blessings, a sage mightsways perchance to generate new chant spells sumday. Universi tranquillo. Paribus paribus.

Types of Spells

hrees be the kindes of spell herein. Evry one holds its owne effect as described. Sum do occur nearby the caster, sum at greate distance. Many spells hold ye secrets not writ in the bok.

Chant Spells may be cast at anytyme, day or night. They be for use by evry being, and be right easy and clear as aer.

Eclipse Spells be mezmero-mystical spells that can only be cast in view of an eclipse. The caster must utter ye lasty wyrd at the peak of the celestial shadow's darkness.

Light Spells are ye most powerful of all ye spells, and shall work for only ye most clevver of casters. Specilais knowing requyrt.

The Greate Forest

Book of LAXT Spells

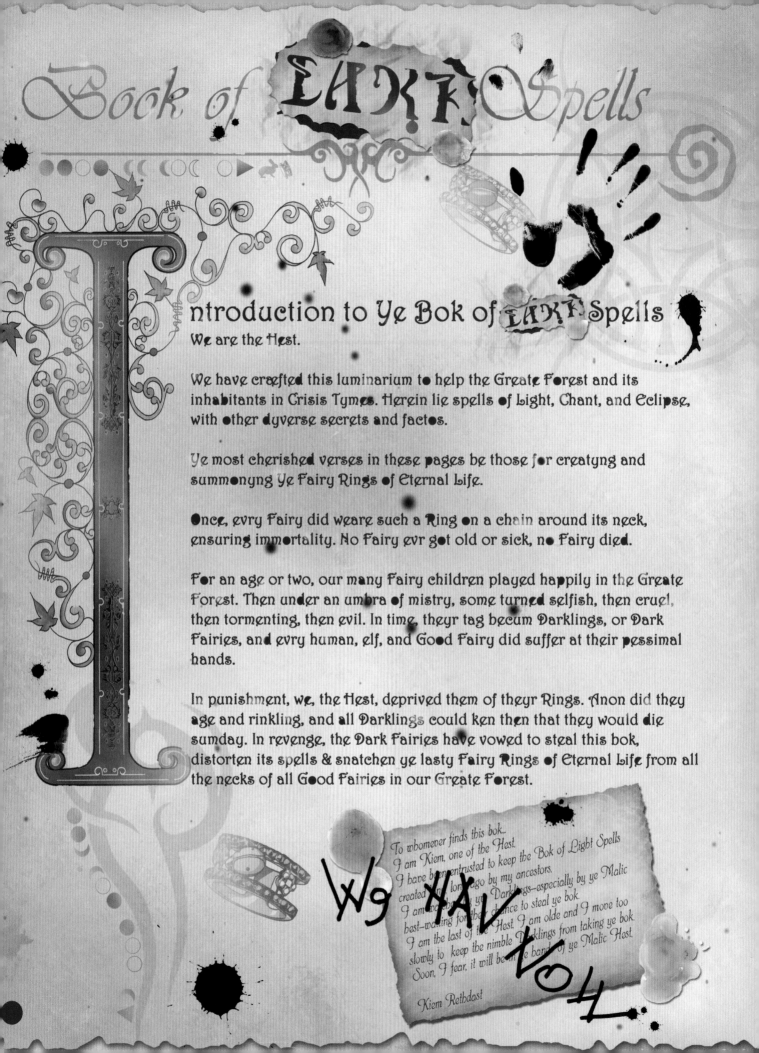

Introduction to Ye Bok of LAXT Spells

We are the Hest.

We have craefted this luminarium to help the Greate Forest and its inhabitants in Crisis Tymes. Herein lie spells of Light, Chant, and Eclipse, with other dyverse secrets and factes.

Ye most cherished verses in these pages be those for creatyng and summonyng Ye Fairy Rings of Eternal Life.

Once, evry Fairy did weare such a Ring on a chain around its neck, ensuring immortality. No Fairy evr got old or sick, no Fairy died.

For an age or two, our many Fairy children played happily in the Greate Forest. Then under an umbra of mistry, some turned selfish, then cruel, then tormenting, then evil. In time, theyr tag becum Darklings, or Dark Fairies, and evry human, elf, and Good Fairy did suffer at their pessimal hands.

In punishment, we, the Hest, deprived them of theyr Rings. Anon did they age and rinkling, and all Darklings could ken then that they would die sumday. In revenge, the Dark Fairies have vowed to steal this bok, distorten its spells & snatchen ye lasty Fairy Rings of Eternal Life from all the necks of all Good Fairies in our Greate Forest.

To whomever finds this bok...
I am Kiem, one of the Hest.
I have been entrusted to keep the Bok of Light Spells created in long ago by my ancestors.
I am hunted by ye Darklings–especially by ye Malic best-wanting for their chance to steal ye bok.
I am the last of the Hest. I am olde and I move too slowly to keep the nimble Darklings from taking ye bok.
Soon, I fear, it will be in the hands of ye Malic Hest.

Kiem Rethdast